It Takes All Sorts

By

The Joined-up Writers Group

Published by YouWriteOn.com, 2011

First Edition

A CIP catalogue record for this title is available from the British Library.

Meet the Authors:

The Joined-Up Writers Group Authors became a working group in 2004 and published their first anthology 'Acorns' in 2006. In the intervening years there have been a few changes to the group, with one or two members withdrawing from activities to be replaced by new writers making the circle a consistent octet.

Maureen Nicholls

Author of **Sylvester**, a children's adventure story published in 2008 by YouWriteOn. A prize winner in several short story competitions and has been short listed for others. Maureen hopes to have the follow up to Sylvester ready for publication by the end of the year.

Jenny Tunstall

Jenny has previously published short fiction in Canada, where she was short-listed for the CBC Annual Literary Awards in 2004. Working in the field of academic publishing, she enjoys the exhilarations of long walks and choral music in her leisure time. She is currently working on a novel set amidst the social changes of 1920s Britain.

Patricia Welford

Born in Birmingham, Mother of three and Grandmother of six has lived most of her life in Worcestershire. An intermittent scribbler until moving to Portishead five years ago. Here she joined a creative writing course and from there the Joined Up Writers Group which encouraged and revitalised her to write for this Anthology.

Ann Merrin

A tutor in Creative Writing for many years, Ann has produced a variety of poems, stories and short plays often inspired by her students for whom, she in turn, is both inspiration and muse.

Patricia Lloyd

Having retired from a career in Social Services Patricia is enjoying writing - mainly short stories and is in the process of putting together a book for her granddaughters. Pat also sings a little, plays piano a little and knits for her granddaughters - a lot!

Alan Beckett

Coming from a background of science and engineering, Alan's experience over the years has greatly influenced his aspirations in the science fiction and fantasy writing genre. Prize winner of a national short story competition and short listed in three local competitions, Alan is now half way through a SciFi/ fantasy novel for children.

Barbara Calvert

Barbara knew she wanted to be a writer from the age of ten. Thirty years as a teacher, encouraging children to love writing, got in the way, but now it's her turn. She has had short stories published and some success in competitions

Jane Mason

With a young family and a busy working life, spare time is a precious commodity for Jane, who regards her writing as an enjoyable hobby. A short story she wrote in 2006 won first prize in a regional magazine competition and she has continued her success by having several more poems and articles published since. A most productive 'hobby'!

You can follow the Joined-up Writers on their web site, using the following link <u>http://joinedupwriters.co.uk</u> and leave comments or chat with any of the authors.

Contents

The Return Of The Ming Dynasty

Maureen Nicholls

I was born, the eldest in a family of six with two younger brothers and three sisters. My father's genes created the strong family resemblance between us all but, whilst I alone was bequeathed the lithe, strong, athletic body of my Dad, my brothers and sisters take after my beloved mother who, it must be said, has the unmistakable tendency to podge.

My childhood was extremely happy despite my father's roaming eye and regrettable penchant for dalliance. In fact, his frequent absences from the family home, far from upsetting my dear mother, came as something of a respite. When Dad was at home, she had little free time for anything other than the fulfilment of his needs, for he was extremely demanding. Once these needs had been met however, he quickly lost interest in the domestic scene and was soon off on his travels. Mum could relax and we children became once more, the most important part of her life.

As young adults, the time came for us to move away from our mother and the family home, each to pursue whatever agenda life had mapped out for us. Learning to live away from Mum and the comfort of our big close-knit family was devastating but the loss of my dearest brother Tai, was very hard to bear, especially as it soon became clear he would be living too far away to allow easy access for visits. However, I lodged with a most accommodating young couple who did everything in their power to make me feel welcome in their home.

There was another lodger in the house at that time, an elderly gentleman named Mr. Boot. At first I found him a little scary but we soon became friends. Indeed it was his friendship helped me overcome my sad bouts of homesickness. He was always jolly and the rather dopey expression in his big kind eyes belied his fierce pugilistic face. Being short in stature myself, I found the opening of doors with high handles very difficult. Mr. Boot on the other hand, thanks to his great height had no difficulty opening any door, no matter what type of handle, high or low, twist or pull. If he ever saw me struggling with a closed door, he never hesitated to open it for me, a kindness I greatly appreciated, especially if it was the door to the fridge or the larder.

My mother taught me that it was good manners to repay a kindness and this I was able to do in a very particular way. Mr Boot, although tall, had difficulty, even at full stretch, in reaching the interesting morsels of food which had been pushed to the back of the kitchen work surface. Being young and agile, it was a simple matter for me to leap up and delicately push the delicious tit bits to the edge where Mr Boot could then reach them easily. Many a midnight feast was shared by the two of us in this way.

Our actions had the added benefit of tidying the surfaces for the kind lady of the house, who in turn, never seemed to mind clearing away the odd broken dish or unwanted wrappings from the kitchen floor, at least, I never happened to be around when she performed this service but I am sure Mr Boot would have told me had it been otherwise.

Although I still missed Tai, life settled into a comfortable pattern. I rose with the sun each day and performed my ablutions with care before leaving the house for work. I was vermin catcher for the neighbourhood and took great delight in presenting each household with the results of my labours. Their screams of appreciation were always thanks enough. I needed no other reward.

There was one occasion however, when the gentleman of the house was so grateful he actually threw an enormous joint of beef to me. I appreciated his kindness but the meat was frozen solid and very heavy; it took a great deal of effort to get it home. It had all been due to my unexpected encounter with a very large black crow. On my way home one morning, I turned a corner and was confronted by this whopping, bad tempered bird, blocking my path. I lunged at it to shoo it away but it only rose a few feet in the air and landed just a short distance further on, still blocking my path. So, I had to repeat the exercise, over and over again until, I have to say, I became very cross. At this point, the wretched thing flew up into the lower branches of a tree and perched there, yelling obscenities at me. It was so rude! Beneath the branches, I stood listening to the appalling sounds issuing from this vulgar bird's beak. It was more than flesh and blood could stand. Taking it completely by surprise, I leapt straight up like a

Massai Warrior and managed to grab it by the tail. I then dragged it, kicking and and screaming through the open door of the nearest house and under the startled and admiring gaze of the neighbour and his wife, I shook it like a rag doll until it stopped swearing.

'There', I told it, 'that'll teach you a lesson' and I let it drop to the floor where it scuttled off into a corner. As I set about cleaning its nasty black feathers from my chest, the man of the house took up the joint of beef, which had been defrosting on the kitchen table and threw it at me. His wife protested that it was their Sunday lunch but he ignored her and I quickly departed with it before he could change his mind; a most successful outcome.

This throwing of gifts soon became commonplace and I began to expect it, rather like a ballerina receiving a thrown bouquet from an admiring audience. One dear lady even gave me her knitting. I had been carefully unwinding the ball of wool for her, being helpful as usual but when she stood up, a strand had caught beneath the chair and the stitches shot off her needles. She said something I didn't quite catch, gathered up the knitting, wrapped it firmly round the ball of wool and threw it at me. I thought it was most kind of her and it made a lovely gift for my landlady who, I must tell you, was most surprised by my generosity.

It was shortly after this that I received the best surprise ever. My brother Tai was to come and live with us. Apparently, Tai's landlady, who was a friend of my landlady, was finding it difficult to cope. I'm not sure why. She informed us that, if she was not to end life in a loony bin, Tai must move out. I got the impression that the poor lady was having marital problems and it is likely that a lodger, however charming, could only be in the way in such a situation. Well, as I loudly told my landlady, this was indeed a happy day for us and, for the neighbourhood as a whole because now, they would have two vermin destroyers for the price of one. Bargain! I immediately took Tai off to show him around and explain the ropes which, being my brother, he was very quick to pick up, as you would expect.

I can't begin to tell you how much I enjoyed his return and what fun we had together. We became the talk of the neighbourhood and people were constantly stopping our landlady to ask about us. She often came home quite pink with embarrassment from some of these encounters. She never found it easy to be praised by her neighbours especially when they called her a saint for looking after us. One neighbour even sent her a special letter after Tai and I had helped rescue her small dog. The poor thing had wandered away from its house one day so, acting as a well honed team, one on each side, we rounded it up and managed to back it up against it's owner's door, where it stood shaking, whilst we called LOUDLY until the owner came to find it. It's nice to do a good turn for people.

The Christmas tree experiment was most memorable! The landlady and her husband argued like crazy about the size of the thing. Mrs said it was ridiculously big and suggested they phone whoever was responsible for putting a tree on the City Centre and offer them ours for free. Mr said that was utter nonsense. He maintained that all he needed to do was chop a few inches off the top and perhaps a foot or so off the bottom. Tai and I watched all this with great interest but made no comment - best not to interfere in a domestic.

After considerable amounts of heaving, and shoving, cutting and swearing, the tree was finally installed in the hall. Mr was exhausted and had to go and have a lie down, leaving Mrs with the 'simple task' of decorating it. This was not without problems because the tree, being so wide was most difficult to get around. In fact, during the whole time it stood in the hall, callers at the front door were requested to 'go round the back', as we couldn't open the front door wide enough to admit a gnat, let alone a person. But I digress.

After considerable effort and perseverance, our dear landlady managed to cover the huge tree with vast quantities of glass balls and fairy lights in a multitude of colours. Sparkly tinsel and hanging silver streamers were then added and, of the utmost interest to Tai and me, at the very top, a robin – a real robin. We decided it must be very tame because it never moved and didn't sing. It was obviously a house robin, not a variety we had ever come across before. SOoo... very interesting.

After such stressful exertion, it was not surprising that the dear landlady needed to stretch out on the settee with a large brandy. Tai and I continued to sit and gaze at the robin. I can't speak for Tai but I gazed with such intensity my blue eyes crossed. We needed to get up to that bird, but how? Crawling under the bottom branches we looked at the stout trunk, rising out of the big bucket and up to the ceiling. We decided it looked thick enough to climb so, Tai ascended on one side and I ascended on the other. At the top, I peered out from beneath the silver tinsel and gazed at the robin. It didn't move. Amazing!

Tai's head popped out from the other side and with incredible agility, he managed to grab the said bird by the tail. Expecting a squawk I braced myself, ready to leap – but - nothing! It was dead! What the hell made them put a dead robin on top of a tree?

Do you know that old saying about curiosity? Well, it darnn nearly was the end of us. The tree started to list sideways and if I hadn't moved pretty sharpish, I would have been crushed beneath when it hit the ground. I leapt to the same side as Tai and together we hung on and rode it like a surfboard on a wave as it crashed to the floor.

A sudden and urgent need for fresh air came over us and we both ran for the garden. Hearts still beating fast but nevertheless, safe and sound, we picked off the pine needles and strolled off down the road in order to calm our shattered nerves. By the time we returned, the tree was back in place but this time, it was firmly tied to a great big hook in the ceiling and the remains of the dead robin were in a paper bag on the hall table.

What a wonderful Christmas that was. We had so much food Tai's belly resembled that of the Buddha figurine which the landlady used to pat for good luck; she soon decided that Tai's belly was even fatter, so patted that instead calling him 'my little Podgebelly,' as she did so.

We listened as the church bells rang out the old year and the fireworks welcomed in the new one. Tai and I thanked the lucky stars which had brought us back together. We curled up next to Mr Boot in front of a roaring fire and watched as the TV commentator raised his glass to wish peace and goodwill to all men. I nudged Tai. 'And to all cats,' I said.

Mr. Boot snored

'And to all dogs, Ming,' Tai added.

I Was The Girl

Jenny Tunstall

I was the girl dressed in gold and green, glitter and sparkle, who opened the act on the high trapeze, that night. Your faces below me were shadowed and blurred, raised in suspense, awaiting your money's worth of thrill. Mine was the playful pendulum swing that hypnotised you all, freezing your smiles into lovely O's of anticipation. I plunged and swooped, glinting and glamorous, bedazzling with light against the gloom of ageing canvas. The heat of the lights and the rush of stale air against my face were nothing once I felt the gusts of your oohs and sighs; and when I flew and curved and somersaulted for you, when I was caught and smiled down at you all, I knew that I'd stopped your hearts for a moment and plugged your breath. Commanding the heart-beat of a crowd; who could ask for more?

I was the girl, black-haired, long-limbed and slender, whose smile never faded, who stretched her arms high in elation as the drum rolled, who floated in ecstasy on the waves of your admiration. I was the girl down in the ring with Alfonso, my hand held high in the hand of the great ring-master himself as he announced the amazing parallel forward and backward triple somersaults that we would perform for you here tonight, ladies and gentlemen, without the aid of a safety net, for your greater wonder and delight. Trumpet fanfare, cheers, applause and my sisters and I climbed the rope ladders as fast as we could, hearts hammering, blood racing.

Bella was adored, our adult sister, tallest, haughtiest, most magnificently decked in gold and blue. Her body had curves despite our mother's best efforts to keep us all skinny and childlike. Bella dreamt of a cottage down by the sea, of hollyhocks and roses and of a heroic and gentle love. Stella wore yellow and tended to puppy fat; she was allowed less food than any of us and craved for more at every hour of day and night. Together we stole from our mother's food cupboard and together we were beaten for it. Together we scorned the

15

rest of the world. Rita in gold and red was far too brittle for our life.
At twelve, she was pale-skinned and built like a sparrow, our half-wit
half-sister, Stella called her, but sometimes I pitied her. She'd have
done well hiding by the sea in Bella's dream cottage. She felt too hard
the bruises and minded too much her father's belt that touched us all
from time to time. He trained us, Fred Thorpe, ignorant sot, and
claimed credit for our act. You were there; you saw it all. Was he
high on the trapeze with us? Was he urging us on from the high
platform or keeping watch from the ringside? Of course not. Never.
Not even when we first performed a new routine. Too busy knocking
our mother about and soaking himself in cheap whisky.

I hated him, of course, but who cared? We got bruises often,
though you never saw them lurking beneath the glitter and sparkle, and
what of it? You didn't need to see the stains of mildew up in the
shadowed heights of the canvas or know that Rowena, the horse-back
artiste, made trouble for us, spiteful bitch, or that Timon, the Strong
Man, terrified us all with his rages. So what if the gold and green
scratched at unfinished seams and reeked of old sweat that would
never wash out of the cloth? Did I care that I was as scared of falling
as the rest of them? I was the one most aware of our mistakes. Mine
was the heartbeat that measured most accurately the recklessness of
our glorious act. But adrenaline flooded through me every time,
intoxicating, exhilarating. I lived for it, the fluttering stomach, the
prickling skin and you made it complete by paying to see me do it; the
biggest dare of all time. I did dare and I was good, the best of the four;
quick eyes, sure hands, fine balance. I was the girl whose body looked
most like a lark in the air. On the ground I was just the third of four
daughters, lost and ignored in the chaos of our muddy lives. And you?
You would have died on my high trapeze. I was immortal the minute I
stepped into the ring, a goddess. It's true. I was the girl, second from
right in the photo they took on our opening night. Not Bella nor Stella
nor Rita Devene, but Greeta, the neater, the sweeter trapeze girl in
green.

I was the one who saw him first. The sting of his whip swung
me round from the cage where the tigers prowled, gold and black,
muscle and claws. Evgeny cursed me in Russian, but I stood my
ground. He was tall and sleek, muscled like his tigers and his golden
hair gleamed in the sunshine. You've never seen anyone so beautiful.

I was the one who saw him scowl at Alfonso, spit on the ground where Fred Thorpe had trodden, hurl wicked-sounding words, even at Timon.

I was the girl bewitched by the man, the one who idolised and worshipped, who watched him sleep, who touched his discarded clothes and breathed his scent. I dreamt nightly of his touch and I would have died for him.

Bella had secrets and I knew them all. She'd furnished a nook of the old store tent and I watched her there sometimes with soft-faced young men from the towns, who fumbled and stroked, who adored her curves and made her gasp like a cooing dove. Only the ones with the smoothest voices and the tenderest smiles were ever invited there. I saw Evgeny watch her, too. I saw him woo her, I saw the contempt and the anger settle on her face and I was the only one who knew how the purple bruise arrived on her cheek.

I was the girl who knew that he watched every night, after shows, as we peeled off the glitter and sparkle. I turned to face him whenever I could, casually dropping my gold and green. How I longed for breasts to catch his eye, for hips like Bella's to swing as I walked.

I was the girl who heard the cries and tiptoed through darkness to the store tent hide. I was the one who heard whimpers and pleas, snarls and grunts, who was transfixed by the gleam of a naked buttock, rising and falling in time to Bella's muffled sobs. I was the girl swamped, melted by desire and I longed for it to be me.

I was the girl first to swing that night, a proud swooping bird to the roll of the drum. I was desperate for glory after a day made miserable by Mother's random beatings, Bella's fault, not ours. Mine was the smile that opened the act as you settled below, with your bag of popcorn and your curiosity stirred. Bella's gold and blue stretched tight over her belly, but our mother was clever even in the midst of fury and none of the fresh bruises showed. Bella's smile was rigid, Stella's made vicious by another day's meals denied and Rita's smile never made it beyond grimace. Mother's pride was shattered. Her beautiful oldest child had ruined her own chances as she'd ruined our mother's seventeen years earlier. Our act and our futures were over, Mother said. Are you surprised that I tossed my head, stretched my arms, pointed my toes with such determination that night? I had everything to prove.

Alfonso was pleased; a full house at last. Half price tickets had brought you all in. There's a smell and a buzz to a well-packed crowd, but Rowena's back-flips left you cold. Ours was the act that brought you to life and I was the girl shining brightest that night. I was the one first caught by the lights, the girl in green and gold.

The music was louder, the drum rolls were longer, Alfonso's proclamations more fanciful than ever; hearts beat harder and you felt the tension. I stretched and pulled, feeling my rhythm, hiding the effort, ignoring the aches, wincing at the crackling of Alfonso's worn out records and the buzz of the loud speakers. I shimmered once more as my gold and green swept slow half-circles high over the ring, to and fro, ebb and flow, high to low, changing positions and watching your faces, like so many pebbles at the bottom of a lake.

We did our single somersaults and simple exchanges first; we did the easy, showy stuff and only when you woke to us did we increase the pace for our marvellous parallel forward and backward triple somersaults, ladies and gentlemen. Tirah lah of the trumpet, prrrr of the drum, first girl flying and turning, turning, turning, reaching and caught. Splutter of applause. Tirah lah of the trumpet. Prrrr of the drum and the second girl flies, turning, reaching and more applause. And now for the parallels. Four girls swing, straining for height, watching, timing, stretching, cheeks reddening, fingers grasping, gold glittering and sparkling. Tirah lah of the trumpet, prrrr of the drum. Two girls flying and turning, turning, turning and reaching far. One is caught. Gasp. Silence. Fingers against fingers slide. Hands grasp air. Time frozen. One girl falling, falling, falling. You saw. You were there.

They taught us to fall silently for the sake of the crowd and she fell without a sound. Three girls swung helpless, watching her fall. She fell for hours until the ring rose to meet her and she sprawled, broken, still, dressed in gold and blue, glitter and sparkle for the very last time.

I was the girl who trained the next day, alone in the tent, pushing my body, ignoring the place where she'd lain. The Police appeared at ten. I slipped from the tent unnoticed and wandered aimlessly, jumping the puddles, shivering, tired. I watched from a distance as Mother packed up the van, Alfonso's final pay in her apron pocket. Rita sat silent and Stella refused food. I went in search of the one person I wanted to see. He was watching Rowena and drawing moodily on a Turkish cigarette when I reached out to stroke that golden head. He turned in a rage, swatted my hand away and drove his fist into my cheek. I reeled with the fire in my face and his foot struck my back the moment I hit the ground. He reached for his whip, but Alfonso was there and they let me go.

I was the girl who should have starred, who should have been billed as the lead of the act. I was the one who hungered the most, who cared the least what else life brought. I was the one who devoted her hours to dazzle, enrapture, to bewitch and entrance, but I was the girl always outshone by Bella. She took what was mine. Fingers slid from fingers. It wasn't my fault. If her timing had been better she'd have lived to this day. What of it? What did you pay to see? A ladies tea-party? A stroll in the park? You knew we could die and she proved the point. I saw her eyes weary and wide. We both saw Evgeny and then her hands reached, desperately short. I offered her mine and my mind went blank; as blank as my heart. I saw bewilderment as she slid away, head jerked back. She didn't grasp, so neither did I. All over in an instant. I never thought she would die. I was left swinging there, upside down, timing gone and I watched your faces, all eyes on her. I hung there long after the others climbed down; just swung 'til momentum died away and the blood settling in my head dimmed my eyes. One girl, dressed in gold and green, glitter and sparkle, show over, glamour gone. I was the girl left dangling alone.

I Am Memory

Patricia Welford

I am memory
A wind whispered wisp
An idea lost but then remembered
Far-flung strands floating to conjoin
The fresh smell of early morning
A kiss so sweet never forgotten
Misty notes of well-loved songs
Moon lit nights, cherished moments
Encompassing smiles for bride and groom
Sighs of Joy with each new babe
Toddler's tale's of enormous import
Children's laughter bright and clear
Happy sunshine days filled full of love
Shady branches, a mighty tree to hug
Rain splashed flowers with petals aglow
Mercy tendered for a broken heart
Then let go each sad event
For more than this am I
For though I'm gone, I still live on
I am memory
I am love

Egyptian Dreams

Ann Merrin

Colin was a beige sort of man. There was nothing outstanding in his looks: pleasant face; salt and pepper hair. He was probably in his fifties, perhaps early sixties. He was the sort of man one might find in a library any day of the week. The sort of man one might ignore any day of the week. But we all have a story and this is his:

'Not many people in today. I pop in most days. They know me quite well in here. Well, that is, Jane and Margaret do. They're the librarians. Always on the lookout for new books for me. They know what I like: Adrienne Wilcox – she's one of my favourites. She writes stories about local stuff. It was through her I met Kerry.
It was funny really. Jane had told me there was a new book in and, I'm blowed, just as I went to reach for it – so did Kerry. Well, of course, being a gentleman I let her take it. We got talking and it turned out she was a real fan as well. We went for a coffee and discussed all the books we'd read. It was lovely to meet someone who knew so much about Adrienne's books. Well, we had a lovely afternoon together and we agreed to meet the following week so that she could pass 'Black Swans' over to me.
And that was it really. 'The start of a beautiful friendship' as they say. We began to meet once a week here in the library. Then we'd go for a coffee in the coffee bar upstairs. We talked about all sorts of things, not just our favourite author. I told her all about me and Mum, and how we'd once met Adrienne when she was doing a bit of research down our street. That was a day to remember that was. Mum invited her in and told her stories about all the neighbours. Adrienne was very interested. I think some of the tales came out in 'Neighbour My Neighbour'. One of her best novels by far. It was all about this woman who nobody liked because she was such a gossip. Well this neighbour is murdered and you just don't know who did it

21

until right at the end – and it turned out that the whole street had been involved! Ooh, it was a good one. Mum didn't rate it
that much, said it was a bit far fetched. Anyway Kerry enjoyed hearing all about it.

Kerry? She's about forty; 5'2'; longish blonde hair (not natural mind, the blonde I mean); lovely blue eyes; dresses a bit like a hippy. Oh, she's a one-off. Always got a smile and an answer for everything. She's a real live wire. She told me all about her travels. Apparently she'd gone travelling with a boyfriend but it didn't work out – he'd gone off and left her with no money. And there she was stranded in Marrakech all on her own. But she lived to tell the tale! Just like her. She got a job on a yacht travelling back to England. Rich family wanted a nanny. I reckon that girl could turn her hand to anything. She lives not far from the library, I'm not sure exactly where. She hasn't got a job at the moment – 'resting' as they say in the theatrical profession. I'm sure it won't be long before she's fixed up though.

It was about Christmastime, I think, that she started to talk about going on a holiday. We talked about places we'd always wanted to visit. Turned out we'd both dreamed of going to Egypt. Funny that. You know, we both loved Adrienne Wilcox who wrote about the local area, but we both longed for distant lands. The desert sand, the pyramids, Arabs and camels, all so far removed from humdrum Eastcombe with its grey skies and drizzle.

For me it was ever since I'd read the Tomb of Tutankamen. I think I'd imagined discovering those tombs myself – that's me, Colin the Intrepid! Kerry said her granddad had been in Egypt during the Second World War and she'd always wanted to see it. We started to look up books about it. This library is great for its geography section. I think Jane and Margaret were quite amused by our enthusiasm over our Egypt project. They ordered several books for us from the Central Library. Nice girls.

She's so interested in everything, Kerry. She made it all come alive. We got maps and planned routes to see all the places of interest – even some we'd never heard of. Then she brought in some travel brochures. The pictures made it look so exotic. We thought the most interesting place looked like the Valley of the Kings.

Well, the long and the short of it is – we decided to go! Yeah, me and Kerry going on a holiday together. Separate rooms, of course.

Though I'm hoping our relationship might develop into something more than just friendship, at a later stage.

It was a bit expensive but Kerry said she'd pay for herself. She'd been saving up. She saw to it all, bless her. I had a bit of money left over from Mum so I thought: Well, blow it, it's not often an old chap would get a chance like this again. Going on an exotic holiday with an attractive young woman.

We paid the deposit in January. Then the full amount was due in March, four weeks before we're due to go. Kerry made sure our passports were all up-to-date. Bless her. I didn't have to do a thing, except get my photos done. She said it was no trouble to her. But that's just like her – nothing is too much trouble. She's done a lot of travelling actually – been all over the world, so she's used to that sort of thing: tickets, passports, foreign money. Second nature to her.

Farthest I've been is Paris. Went there with Mum not long before she died. Ooh but we did have a good time. I'd never seen her looking so young and full of fun. She'd had a hard time since Dad left, but once we got off that coach, she really let her hair down. We went up the Eiffel Tower; cruised on the Seine; drank wine and everything. I'm glad we went. Who'd have thought she'd be dead two months later. That's three years ago now and I still miss her. But 'life goes on and we must go with it', as she used to say. She was a great one for sayings my Mum. I don't know what she'd be saying now though, at the thought of her son going off to Egypt with a young woman.

It was quite exciting handing over that cheque. £800. A lot of money, but it meant that we were really going. That was two weeks ago. Kerry hasn't been in since then. I expect she's busy packing, only another two weeks to go. I haven't had my tickets yet. I don't know if Kerry has had hers. It's a shame I don't know where she lives or I could just pop in and see her. Still I come in here most days, just in case she's been in.

Jane said she had tried to contact Kerry but her letter had been returned 'not known at this address'. I think she was quite cross because Kerry still has two Adrienne Wilcox books out and they're overdue now.

She said she'd let me know if Kerry does come in. She'll phone me. And of course Kerry knows my address. I come in anyway, I like it here. I'll pop in again tomorrow.'

Colin may not be a wise man but he still has his dreams.

The Homecoming

Patricia Lloyd

He felt the ship shudder as the sails furled. The ship was slowing as it neared the end of its journey. Sean could just make out through the sea mist, Cobh dock from where he had sailed fifteen years before. Was this the right thing to do - to return after so long? Fear surrounded his heart, the heart that had yearned to return every day he had been away. Would she still want him?

The dock didn't look too different. There were a few more buildings, many more ships and if anything, it was certainly a good deal busier. He had left Ireland on 9 September 1833. After four months in Galway jail and a travesty of a court case, he had been sentenced to transportation for life to Australia.

While he was away Daniel O'Connell had fought (through parliament) for equality of land rental and ownership and the end of the Irish Tithe System. Was he returning to a fairer and a more just Ireland?

What of Maureen? They had been married for two years when he was sent away. Connor was just beginning to walk and seemed to spend a great deal of time holding on to his mother's skirts for balance. He smiled remembering the little boy trailing his mother around the kitchen, never for a moment letting go of that skirt which was all that kept him from falling. For a moment he remembered the heart-wrenching agony of leaving them.

Maureen had written. Her letters had taken weeks to reach him but he had heard from her three or four times a year. She had kept the cottage and land even though he had been deported for threatening the landowner. Probably Lord Carstairs had not wanted any more repercussions after the court case. He, like many landowners had started to reclaim the land they had previously let to their workers. This was because the grazing of sheep gave a greater financial reward. Workers had rebelled against this move as they used the land they rented to grow vegetables to feed their families and augment their low pay.

Carstairs had served notice for the return of the land Sean and his forebears had cultivated for generations. Sean had visited the big house to plead his case that without the land on which to grow food, he would be unable to feed his wife and child. After a fierce row Carstairs called his men and had Sean thrown out. Later that day Sean was arrested. He never saw his home again. He saw Maureen in the court room, but they were not allowed to see each other before he sailed for Australia.

Sean's thoughts returned to the present as, on dry land once more and waiting for his bags to be unloaded from the ship, he wondered what means of transport he could hire to take him the twelve miles to Maureen. Enquiring at a chandlery he was able to hire a horse – arranging for his bags to follow by horse and cart the following day.

He mounted the horse and settled into the saddle. Gently bringing the horse under control, his spirits lifted. He would be with them again soon. What would she think? Had she found someone else? Was she still living in the cottage? It had been six months since he last heard from her.

He set his horse to walking out of the dock area and followed the road as it climbed the hill taking him to the coast path which would eventually take him home.

What would she say when she saw him ride up on a horse? She would probably take him for gentry. What would she say when he explained that after all these years he had been pardoned and given his freedom from the sheep station on which he had worked since arriving in Australia? What would she say when he told her that he had made a great deal of money from managing and eventually owning his own sheep and cattle ranch? All the skills he had learned working the estate of Lord Carstairs had made him very employable in Australia. Would she want to return to Australia with him? He remembered the love they had shared. When they married, it had been for ever. Their commitment had been total. She was his heart and soul. Did she still love him after all this time?

The light was fading as he made his way along the lane which led to the cottage. As he dismounted and tied the horse to a nearby tree, no-one came from the house.

He walked around to the back of the house. In a distant field he could see a woman and boy. Was it a boy or young man? If this was Connor he was head and shoulders taller than his mother. They were planting. Every now and then they stood as if to ease an aching back. The woman was slim and willowy – the gazelle he had always compared her to. Her waist was still trim – emphasised by the sacking apron she wore.

He was suddenly shy. How did he approach them? Did they want him? As he hesitated, the boy looked up and called something – probably asking what he wanted. He began to walk towards them.

The woman – his Maureen – stood, flexed her back and turned to see who was coming. He saw her stiffen with disbelief. Is it? Can it be? Then she was running, running towards him as he ran to her. When she reached him she stopped him with hands to his chest and looked at him closely. For minutes she looked at his eyes, his hair, his nose, his lips over and over again. She then took his face between her hands and said, 'I have been waiting for you. I have missed you with all my heart. I have never stopped loving you'. Then she jumped up to reach him as he enveloped her in his arms and kissed her.

In the lane nearby, the local parson saw the man and woman kissing so blatantly where all could see and tutted in despair at their undignified behaviour. He saw the woman call the boy to her. He saw the boy shake the man's hand and then the man reach for him hugging him to his heart. As he carried on up the lane he saw all three of them walking in a line, arms around each other, towards their cottage.

Hamadryad

Alan Beckett

Do you not wince when the long boughs sway,
when the winds caress your branched bark,
twisting your sacred temple this way
and that. Do you not cry from the heart?

You're truly damned, sewn in your bower.
How is it that you endure the gales
of life's thrusting, corrupting power,
when you are so defenceless and frail?

Is the tree of years your secret cross
with its entangled limbs, vines entwined?
Never in fear of arboreal loss.
So, I will drink deep from love's sweet wine.

Morphed spirit who dwells in the aired leaves
bound to the Earth. Are you not that first
heart beat, that quivering thump that breathes
love into the hearts of men, to burst.

So embraced, so bonded to your tree
and yet so happy though still as ice.
There's nought twix Hamadryad and me
for my love's love too will demand her price.

The Last Piece

Barbara Calvert

D. I. Philip Barlow had been in the Force for more than twenty years but that feeling of frustration that hovered around at the beginning of a new case had never quite left him. For the past ten minutes he'd been sitting at his desk, the door to his office unusually closed, just staring ahead at the notice board that covered most of the opposite wall. In the centre, two pictures of Alice Miller stared out at him. The largest was a 10 inch by 7 inch studio photograph. According to her parents it was taken on her birthday just over a year ago. He could still picture her mother's tortured face as she had handed it to him the day after Alice's body had been discovered. And this thought led him to the second picture; Alice as she had been found; naked, on the bathroom floor, her head smashed on the ceramic surround of her shower cubicle. The fact that Alice had been such an attractive girl, with her long blond hair, smooth flawless skin and bright smiling eyes, made her death seem that much more tragic. He knew this wasn't fair. He liked to think that even if the body had been that of an overweight, greasy haired, spotty youth this feeling of regret would have been the same, but he knew it wouldn't.

At that moment a knock on the door jolted him out of these quiet reflections and Detective Sergeant Laura Scott, his second in command on this case, put her head round the door to ask if he was ready for the team briefing. On the day that Alice's body had been found, he hadn't expected that they'd be needing a team to deal with the incident. Back then it looked as though it would turn out to be a straightforward case of misadventure; soon cleared up and handed over to the coroner.

'Give me ten minutes.' Barlow turned away from the board. 'I need to get my head round this one.'

The office display board was the focus of his deliberations. Phil Barlow saw it like a giant jigsaw puzzle, and already there was a scattering of pieces across the board. The two photos took up the centre, Alice before and Alice after. His challenge was to sort out the in-between. He'd never been a jigsaw enthusiast but he could still remember family Christmases when 'doing a puzzle' was one of the well-worn ways of passing the time. First the border, with the straight edge pieces and specially the four corners, then the difficult bit; filling in the middle. All the notes, reports and photographs of the scene, were already on the board, creating a border made up of facts; the truths that went only a small part of the way to explain what had really happened to Alice.

When her parents had contacted the police with their concerns it was because they'd not been able to get in touch with their daughter. It was so unlike her and they were so far away. They were getting very worried.

'How old is she? 25? What planet are they on? A twenty five year old, not at home, mobile probably left in some bar or other, gone off with some Romeo for a couple of nights' recreation I expect. We've got quite enough on the go without looking for work. Tell them to contact as many of her friends as they can, and her work colleagues. Ring us back if they get any further information.' Barlow had come across their type before, the over-anxious parent. 'We won't hear from them again.'

But they had. Later that day they phoned again and this time it was Laura Scott who had spoken to them. Not much older than Alice herself and a long way from her parents, she managed to find a couple of uniformed officers who happened to be in the area so she could send them to take a look at Alice's flat. When their knocking and bell ringing brought no response, and when, looking through the letterbox, they could clearly hear music playing, they decided that action was needed. Breaking a small glass panel at the side, they soon had the door open and it hadn't taken them long to discover Alice's body in the bathroom. It looked like a straightforward accident: a case of slipping on a wet floor. But something just hadn't felt right.

By the time an ever-so-slightly remorseful Barlow had arrived at the house, things had moved on swiftly. The scene of crime officers had been brought in and the blue and white tape stretching across the foot of the stairs suggested that all was not as it had first appeared. SOCO had discovered at least four faint, but distinct, large, seemingly male footprints, on the landing carpet leading away from the bathroom and again on the top four treads of the stairs.

'We'll be able to match the traces left on the carpet with those on the bathroom floor, but I'll put money on it that whoever wore those shoes was in that room.' Jim Burton, the SOCO had sounded pretty confident, and was later proved to be absolutely right.

The forensic pathologist had confirmed that Alice had been dead for at least 48 hours and that it was the blow to her head that had caused massive internal bleeding. Death would have been pretty much instantaneous. But he too doubted that it was an accident. For one thing it seemed that Alice's hair was still coated in shampoo and yet the shower had been turned off. Why would she have turned off the water and stepped out of the shower without rinsing her hair? And then there was her bathrobe. This lay on the floor, partly across her legs, the towelling loop broken. Had she grabbed at it, hanging from the nearby hook, tearing the loop as she fell? There were, however, no signs to suggest that Alice had been assaulted or that there had been any struggle.

'This lock hasn't been forced.' Jim Burton pointed to the wooden door surround, 'Not a scratch or a scrape anywhere on the paintwork. Whoever was there when Alice died had either been let in or had let themselves in, and then let themselves out again presumably.'

These were the facts, and also the questions, that made up the so far, incomplete puzzle on Barlow's notice board. And the answers? Barlow ran through in his mind his own version of what had happened. Alice was in her shower, someone came into the bathroom, she stepped out of the shower, reaching in panic for her bathrobe, slipped and fell. Whoever had surprised her must have turned off the shower, before leaving her, lying there on the floor, possibly, at that moment, still alive. Yes. In his mind this part of the puzzle was complete but some vital pieces were still missing. Who was it who had invaded her privacy? Who caused this panic and then left her for dead?

Barlow called the team into his room. The purpose of this meeting was to bring together all the information that the team members had gathered.

Sue Taylor, one of the support staff, had a special job. Every piece of information, no matter how insignificant, would have to be recorded on a Post-it and added to the board. Barlow stood alongside, and as he talked, and invited ideas from his team he moved the yellow squares around searching for connections.

Barlow and DS Scott had talked to the last people to see Alice alive, her three friends, Clare, Debbie and Ruth. They had spent a 'girly' evening at Alice's flat, watching a DVD, drinking a couple of bottles of wine and 'chilling out'. They had left Alice at 11.30pm, after clearing away the debris of the occasion. Alice had already started to prepare for bed.

Barlow himself had spoken to Alice's parents, when they had arrived from their home a couple of hundred miles away. They kept in regular contact with their daughter and had no idea of any worries that Alice might have had. Her boyfriend of three years was in Australia, where he had been for the past three months and was due back within weeks. As far as they knew there were no difficulties and neither her friends nor her family believed that she had become involved with anyone else. Everyone described Alice as friendly, happy and busy.

On his first visit to the crime scene Barlow had noticed her key, lying on the small table near the door. The door had a Yale type lock and a bolt, which had not been put across. Attached to the key ring was a house-shaped fob bearing the name 'Carruthers and Rowe – Estate Agents'. This had immediately rung alarm bells. There had been previous cases where estate agents had been targeted by bogus potential buyers as they showed them around properties. Perhaps Alice had unknowingly become the victim of an obsessional client. Further enquiries at Carruthers and Rowe, however, established that Alice's work involved commercial properties only and that she very rarely met individual clients alone, and certainly there were no records of any such activities in the past six months.

Detective Constables Kevin Ledbury and Conrad Farr had visited the other tenants in the apartment block where Alice lived. Of the six apartments, four residents had been at home on the night of Alice's death. The fifth, Mrs Audrey Fry, who lived in the flat opposite Alice's, had been in hospital for the whole of the previous week and her flat had been empty. No-one reported anything unusual on that night; they had heard nothing significant, although the Clarks in the flat below had heard Alice's friends leave and confirmed the time at about 11.30. They had both been reading in bed at the time.

Post-it notes were now dotted around the board and Barlow began to group them together in an attempt to build up small, clear pictures of the separate parts of Alice's life. What he was looking for was a link; a piece out of place or an unusual fitting together; a small piece of information that might link two apparently unconnected pieces. But they needed more action. Ledbury and Farr reported that Mrs Fry had been released from hospital the previous day so Barlow decided to pay her a visit. She had not been there on the night of Alice's death but, as the resident living closest to Alice, she just might have that special piece of information that would connect up all those seemingly unrelated facts.

Mrs Fry's middle-aged daughter, who had come to stay with her for a few days, opened the door to Barlow and Scott. Before taking them into the sitting room she explained quietly that her mother had been very distressed by the news of the 'terrible tragedy', and asked that they handle her very sensitively. Barlow explained what they would be talking about and reassured her that they would take no more than half an hour. As it turned out Mrs Fry had very little to contribute. She knew Alice well as a neighbour. She backed up everyone else's view of her as a kind, happy, friendly young woman. Before her hip operation, when she had found it difficult to get around, Alice had done little bits of shopping for her; had sometimes stopped to have a cup of tea, but not often, as she always seemed to be busy with one thing or another. In just twenty minutes Barlow and Scott had all the information they were going to get. Mrs Fry's daughter led them to the door. D.S. Scott noted the hooks fixed onto the wall next to the door, and made a mental note to advise Mrs Fry, at some time in the future, that it wasn't a good idea to have keys so easily accessible. Phil noticed this too, but his eyes were fixed on a key attached to a ring bearing a house-shaped fob.

'Could I go back to have another word with your mother?' he asked, already halfway to the sitting room. 'Mrs Fry did you have a key to Alice's flat?'

The keys Barlow had noticed were indeed Alice's. She had been known to lock herself out from time to time and had felt safer knowing that there was a spare key with Mrs Fry.

'Could you tell me who has a key to your flat Mrs Fry?' The spark was igniting. Could this be that missing piece?

It was Mrs Fry's daughter who answered, ' Well I have one and so does Jason. He's my son. He lives closer, just around the corner. It's easy for him to pop in to check up on mum, especially when she wasn't too well, with her hip you know.'

Things moved quickly after that and Barlow, though he would never admit it, was quite impressed at how everything fell into place. The grandson's housemates couldn't account for his whereabouts on the night of Alice's death, and when presented with this, Jason Langton gave up any attempt to deny his involvement in Alice's death. He'd got to know Alice from his visits to his grandmother, and, though she'd always been pleasant to him, it was very clear that she was not interested in taking this any further. His obsession with Alice had built up over months, although Alice seemed totally oblivious to it. None of her friends had ever heard her mention him. With his grandmother in hospital he was given that irresistible access to the key to Alice's flat. For what reason, and what he had intended to do once there, he made no attempt to explain. He had surprised Alice in her shower and the rest of the story was just as Barlow had imagined it.

Now Barlow was preparing his report for the Crown Prosecution Service. It would be down to them to decide the precise charge to be brought. He paused, put down his pen and stared again at his jigsaw board. He picked up the pad of yellow 'stickies' from his desk. He wrote the final piece of information that completed the puzzle and he was reminded of the last piece of the jigsaw from his childhood Christmases that had quite often slipped, unnoticed, under the table.

Survival Instinct

Jane Mason

A grey metal framed window, containing solid iron bars, was standing between her and freedom. Along the perimeter of the grounds, a mini digger was noisily carving out a new landscape to gaze upon. If she were unlucky enough to still be here, once it was completed, then she would be able to stroll around the new garden.

A French cigarette, being smoked somewhere in the room, wafted its' enticing aroma towards the ceiling in a hazy blue pall. Antoine danced lovingly into her view. He was doing that more and more lately. His dark moustache was set above a rich enticing mouth, unforgettable but unreachable except from within. He'd broken her heart.

The doctors told her the condition was treatable with time, rest and plenty of therapy, but what did these youngsters know? Her thick veined hands reached out and clasped Antoine's face, tracing perfectly every detail exactly as she remembered them. A warm wet sensation oozed out from beneath her plaid skirt. Too late, oh how annoying. 'Nurse, nurse I need your help', she pleaded, remaining seated on the pink velour sofa.

'Mrs Cooper, have you had another little accident?'

Wasn't that what happened when someone was injured or died? This was just a natural everyday occurrence surely.

The long winding corridors and locked doors reminded her of a previous life. They didn't wear black boots here but the constant questioning was the same. Over and over, repeating, tell us this, tell us that, how do you feel about this and that?

Tap, tap, tap, her fingers played her never forgotten tune, specifically coded.

'Cup of tea Mrs Cooper?' enquired the nurse breaking her concentration.

'Yes dear, that would be lovely thanks'. The familiar pitying glance, that nurse couldn't make proper tea anyway.

Aaah! She firmly placed her hands over both ears. The noise was deafening. Antoine was begging. Too late the bullet lodged between his eyes, he fell backwards, whilst bits of brain splattered the wall behind him. She was calm, watchful, waiting. The black booted man lifted her up off her feet and pushed her towards the waiting vehicle.

'Mrs Cooper, are you alright?'

Was she? Of course she was, she had to be. Strong and upright, ready to save them all. She couldn't let the side down.

Night time came and laying in bed her parachute had somehow become wrapped around her body. She couldn't breathe, she was panicking. She pressed the red button, so as they could cut the strings and release her.

'Not again Mrs Cooper, you can't keep falling out of bed, you'll do yourself an injury if you're not careful.'

'Too late for that dear', she muttered.

Morning arrived at last and with it news of a great grandchild. Her son in law had phoned to say, her granddaughter Sarah, had given birth to her first great granddaughter Eva. Her heart lifted at the thought of being able to hold a wonderful new baby in her arms again. This was why she had to get better, repair herself, mend whatever was broken. Her future was beckoning, wishing to comfort her. Unfortunately the past still had to be dealt with.

Jack, her son had come to visit her. 'Mum it's good to see you. Are they looking after you in here?'

Jack, standing so straight, tall and trusting, Jack, the clever one going off to university straight from school, attaining an education and now running an accountancy practice. Such a typically British name as well. He needed to know, she needed to tell him, but how?

'Congratulations Jack, its wonderful news about Sarah and little baby Eva. Is the baby's name permanent or is there still time to change it?'

'Why would Sarah want to change it Mum?' I think it's a beautiful name.

'Yes it is Jack, but there's something I need to tell you about my youth, that may affect the naming of the baby.'

'Go on, I'm sure it can't be anything that bad.'

Drawing in a deep raspy breath, she began to recount her days in France as a radio operator, her underground work with the resistance, her special time with Antoine.

Then the horrendous capture and finally the way in which she had managed to secure her passage from France, fraternising with the enemy. She looked deep into his pale blue eyes for acceptance. Did he understand her properly, his parentage and why the name held such powerful bad memories?

Eva Brown was not a name she wanted in her family. She hoped he fully understood her now.

Friends Come and Go

Ann Merrin

I once had a friend called Martha
She was pretty and funny and slim
When we all went to the wine bar
Martha was off to the gym

She was the one with her own house
A car with a new number plate
When we all went to a nightclub
Martha always picked up the date

So Martha the stunner was too good
Too good to keep as a friend
But we needn't have felt so inferior
Her reign was coming to an end

This is how it happened
On the occasion of a girl's night out
Martha met Jed the slime ball
And she fell for the smarmy lout

It was the beginning of the end for Martha
She married Jed the cad
In no time she had four children
And her teeth had all gone bad

She drove around in a pick up
And she'd put on a lot of weight
Her clothes were all from Oxfam
And her hair was a right old state

I don't see much of Martha now
I've got my own house you see
I drive around in a brand new car
We go clubbing the girls and me

I suppose the moral of this story is:
Your world may feel abundantly rich
But don't be too complacent
Because life can be such a bitch

The Accomplice

Patricia Welford

It was a lovely morning for being outside. The blackbird was trilling out his song and the sparrows in the hedge nearby competed with their noisy chattering. Eddy paused in his digging to listen to their happy sounds. He certainly needed cheering up. Bending again determined to finish the post hole he put his foot to the spade and the rhythm continued, down into the earth the blade bit, levelling out full of soil, lift and turn the shaft, up and over the side emptying. With each movement his conscience whispered, matching his rhythm, mur – der – er. Again, the spade dug into the loam, fill and out, mur- der- er. Eddy threw his spade down and wiped his brow. He needed Tom to arrive, Tom's bright and happy face was all he needed to bring him out of his guilt.

He looked back towards the houses, a pair of semis, his own and Tom and Betty's. Recently a widower Tom had agreed to sell the bottom of his garden to Eddy just keeping back a narrow lane down to the coastal path. This had allowed Eddy to widen his much loved vegetable patch considerably. Yesterday and today had been set aside to fence in the new boundary. Just then, the sound of Tom's back door slamming reached Eddy's grateful ears and Tom came into view crunching down the gravel towards him.

'Hello Tom, lovely morning,' Eddy called

'Yes isn't it. Just the job for finishing the fencing, I'm glad we picked the wicker panels it will look really nice.' Tom arrived at the side of the hole. 'Now what do you want me to do?'

'This is nearly finished. One more spadeful should do it. If you could bring the post over we can concrete it in.'

Fetching the last but one post over, Tom then returned for the wheelbarrow of concrete.

'Ready?' He enquired, lifting some of the wet mix on his spade.

41

'Yes I have it straight now.' Eddy stood a little to the side of the post, holding it firm as Tom shovelled the concrete in until it was level with the ground.

'Shall we have our break ? I've brought a flask down from the house?'

'Why not?' Glad to see you are looking so much better these days Tom, and you shovelled that concrete like a fifty year old, great stuff to see.'

They both sat down and a companionable silence stretched between them. Eddy knew that this would be when Tom dropped off to sleep, but he did not mind, he was so pleased to see his old friend getting stronger by the day, enjoying his life. He had been treated like a slave by that nagging bitch Betty. Yes, he thought, if I hadn't acted when I had, it would have been Tom dead not her.

The morning sun shone down on the two men and before long with the warmth and the silence encompassing them, Tom went to sleep. While Tom slept, Eddy's thoughts returned to sitting in the garden ten years before with his dad Stan who was pressing a phial into his hand.

'Do you believe in euthanasia, Eddy?' his dad had asked

'Never really thought about it.' Eddy looked from the phial to his dad thoughtfully.

'Well as time passes you may find that the question arises and tests you. I hope it never does, but when I saw your mother in so much pain, I was glad she and I had talked it over.' He pointed to the bottle which Eddy was now holding up to look at. 'This little phial helped her go when she was ready and no one ever knew.' Stan's voice trembled with emotion as he continued. 'Eddy, I want you to do the same for me if the need arises. All you need to do is mix it with almond oil and spread a very little on my arm. As the oil warms, the poison will be absorbed through my skin passing into the blood stream. It will send me into a deep sleep first then cause my heart to stop. I won't know anything about it. It is untraceable after death so they'll think I have had a heart attack.'

'Dad!' Eddy exclaimed thunderstruck.

'No listen to me son, don't say anything.' Stan leaned over and placed a calming hand on Eddy's arm. 'It probably won't be necessary. I will most likely die in my bed with my boots on. Come on cheer up. Will you promise me to keep it secret and safe?'

Eddy was too shocked and numbed to do more than nod briefly.

'Now this one son,' Stan produced another phial from a deep pocket. 'Is for use should someone find the oil and be stupid enough to use any. It is the antidote but it has to be ingested within an hour.'

'Where did they come from?'

'The native Burmese people during the war Eddy, when I was one of the few escapees under cover, that's where. We got a few of the invaders I can tell you quietly and efficiently. It's one of the few things I managed to do during that filthy campaign.'

Fortunately, for Eddy, his father did die in his bed and the phials had remained hidden at the bottom of a trunk with the old soldier's medals. Eddy had kept them for his own demise should he feel the need, but now decided Tom's need was greater.

It had taken a while to sort everything out, but with the antidote at hand, he had eventually come up with a plan. During this time he had seen Tom getting more and more miserable losing his spirit to carry on, fading away under the barrage of demands and the haranguing Betty gave him. Tom was always worried about money as she 'kept up with the Jones'; the latest of this and the latest of that.

Of course Eddy could only guess what actually happened in the house that day, He was very nervous when he went into Tom 's house to make sure everything had gone to plan, but Betty had been dead alright so there had been no going back.

Humbug, Betty's cat, had been a necessary accomplice. He hadn't been able to think of any other way, but Humbug had survived the experience with little side effect. The warmth of the late morning began working its charms on him too, he relaxed and dozed, slipping into his recurring dream of that fateful day. It was in his dream that the cat's part became real.

Humbug, walked sleepily through the cat flap. It had been a good day overall. The summer sun had shone brightly and he had sought dappled shade on the coast path for most of the morning. On his return journey through Mr Next Door's garden he was pleasantly surprised to be greeted by Mr Next Door who offered a piece of chicken. He really felt very contented, a morsel of chicken had been just the ticket after his long walk and to cap it all Mr Next Door had spread oil on his back, very unusual. Very strange his sleepy brain registered, but there's no accounting for folk, just for fun, he supposed. Anyway, he had licked some of it off but it made his coat feel wonderfully soft, he hadn't removed it all, his treacle and black striped coat gleamed with a wonderful sheen.

Now as he looked about him in the spotless kitchen he heard the click of his mistresses' heels as they passed through the hall on their way to the lounge. He nosed his dish, which held an assortment of treats, fish and another bit of chicken teased his senses. He ate nothing however, he really was too tired and satisfied after calling in on Mr Next Door. He wandered into the lounge where his mistress was sitting down on the sofa.

'There you are where have you been?' His mistress chided him. Walking over to him, she picked him up and sat down again. Humbug settled on her lap, and began to purr, giving way to the peaceful stroke of her hand as it passed gently along his back. Betty settled down to relax with her beloved Humbug. He really was the only thing she had truly loved, and she stroked his lovely fur until she fell asleep.

Obviously Betty was unaware that Eddy had spread poisoned almond oil on Humbugs coat, also lacing the chicken that the cat had enjoyed with the antidote ensuring that the animal would not share his mistress's fate. Humbug had gone into a near comatose state, his purr changing into a gentle snore. Betty however had long ceased stroking her darling's lovely fur. Her breathing had slowly stopped, her hands now still, her head slumped down over her chest. Betty was dead.

Humbug woke up as Betty's hand fell away from his back, he slowly jumped down and returned through the back garden to see if Mr Next Door had any more chicken, he felt really hungry again and very very thirsty.

Still half-asleep, Eddy realised that he had been dreaming as he recalled seeing Humbug that day unsteadily shuffling back down the path, quickening his pace as he spotted Eddy.'

'OK old fellow?' he had enquired, using his gloved hand to caress him. 'Want some more of my special chicken? But you have to be bathed first my lad, all that oil needs removing from your fur before you lick any more off, we don't want your master to see you in this state.'

Eddy sighed dismissing the memory. He hoped that in time his guilt would fade. Murderer his conscience repeated for the second time today.

'No!' said Eddy out loud.'

'What's that?' Tom murmured waking slowly.

'Oh nothing, I must have dropped off myself,' Eddy smiled at his friend.

'Look we've let our tea go cold. Never mind I'll get a fresh pot brewed up and then we'll finish the fence posts so tomorrow we can attach the panels. I'm really looking forward to seeing it finished Eddy.'

'It's very good of you to sell me this piece of land Tom.'

'Nonsense, the money will be very useful. I would have sold it before but you know that I couldn't while Betty was alive; I never did understand why she wouldn't part with it. After all, I couldn't manage it anymore and we still have access to the coastal path, not that she ever went down, she just wanted to sit in the house all day fussing Humbug. He was all she seemed to care about, he added sadly, bending down to his cat giving him a loving stroke. 'Just you and me now old boy.

'I know Betty could be cruel and bitter', Tom continued, 'but she never was to you old chum, was she?' Tom straightened up, turning back to Eddy as he did so. 'He really was clever in letting you know something was wrong on that dreadful day, wasn't he? I wouldn't have survived the shock if I'd come home and found her myself. I know she wasn't the best of people but it was a shame that her end came on the one day when I went to the hospital for my check up.'

'I know,' Eddy replied, 'but she died peacefully in her sleep. The doctor told you she wouldn't have known anything about it.'

'I would only say this to you.' Tom moved closer softening his voice. 'But my life's so calm without Betty always ordering me about, demanding new things all the time. I was always worrying where the money was coming from. I'm feeling so much better in myself.' Tom stood up; spread his arms out enthusiastically his voice strengthening to a shout. 'I feel reborn.'

'I can tell Tom, I can tell' Eddy laughed, 'How about that cup of tea you promised me.'

As Tom returned to his house, Eddy watched him go with tears in his eyes. At his feet, the cat, languorous and stretching in the sun, mewed. He crouched beside him whispering.

'I'm an executioner Humbug old fellow and you, my unknowing accomplice, helped me but I'm the one, who has to learn to live with my conscience. As surely as I killed Betty, her tenacious bullying was killing your master, robbing him of his will to live. Oh Humbug, an executioner I may be but not a murderer, I'll never admit to that. Never.'

Pillow Talk

Alan Beckett

Wayne could not sleep. He sat up on one elbow and looked around the room. Maybe it was the new bed he thought to himself. He hoped not. It had cost an absolute fortune. Dynamic spring tensioning, micro-massaging, individual memory contouring, dust proof, stain proof, mite proof and probably sleep proof he whispered into the darkness of the bedroom. He leaned over towards Gale. She was asleep. Wayne elbowed her to make sure.

'Just my luck,' he lamented. 'Pity this technological wonder-bed can't button her noise up as well,' he grumbled under his breath, somewhat uncharitably. Gale was snoring like an elephant with shredded sinuses but despite that seemed to be dead to the world. It's usually her that has the trouble getting her beauty sleep, Wayne thought. He took a closer look at his reclining, curlered wife. 'Mind you. It doesn't seem to be working much,' he quietly guffawed to himself.

Wayne flopped back onto the bed and shut his eyes. 'She's well away in noddy-land. Typical!' he said under his breath. Normally, after a few lagers I don't have any problem sleeping,' he grieved, not even attempting to try and lower his voice. He turned over, burped and then turned again. He could not settle. He supposed that any moment now he would have to get up and point Percy at the porcelain.

'Why the hell can't I sleep?' he reflected in a much less than cheery disposition. He was about to shift his position yet again when there was a noise. He froze. The sound started up again. He sat up on one elbow and looked into the blackness. It was the sound of rushing water.

'Oh my gawd. The tank's gone,' he screeched at Gale. But she slept on.

After a few seconds, the noise changed into the sound of wind blowing through trees, and then it stopped. Apart from Gales rhythmic snoring all was quiet again.

'Jeese! What was that?' Wayne exclaimed, clearly disturbed. He could not begin to guess what was going on with the central heating to cause such weird noises. He then thought he had heard someone's voice.

'Pardon, dear,' he enquired sweetly, thinking that Gale had just said something; but she continued snoring. After a moment he shrugged his shoulders and flopped back on the pillow.

Suddenly, close by, a woman's voice whispered again in a low and seductive manner. 'I'm here to relax you and I will show you the way......'

'Whoa!' Wayne whooped.' Sitting bolt upright he looked down at his wife. 'Jeese, Gale. Was that you?' His wife moaned sleepily. Turning away from him she continued snoring. 'Oh Gawd! There are voices in me head now,' he gesticulated as his popping eyes pierced the unyielding darkness of the room in abject horror.

'Just let your tired body sink down and mould itself into the sheets. Imagine that ……..'

'Agh!' shouted Wayne. This time he jumped out of bed, thumped to the ground and proceeded to blunder about, stubbing his toes into various items of furniture, and hitting ornaments that had been positioned, for reasons known only to his wife, at strategic impact points around the room. Gale slept serenely on.

'Jeese! Jeese!' bellowed Wayne, now in an advanced state pain and trepidation. He was waving a hastily acquired umbrella at the would be trespasser. Any thoughts as to what an umbrella was doing in the bedroom at that moment of extreme creepiness, was beyond him. 'Who are you? What do you want?' he squeaked, stabbing the wall above the head-board.

'All I want is for you to just relax and join me on a very special journey into your imagination,' answered the woman's soft, enticing voice.

'What!' replied Wayne, slicing the air with his umbrella sword. 'Who the hell are you?' he cried out.

'I'm your bloody wife!' barked Gale, now clearly awake and exceedingly annoyed.

48

'There's a bleeding ghost behind our bed. Listen.'

Gale sat up and listened intently for a moment or two. She then began to laugh and wheeze pointing at her husband's quivering form.

'Idiot!' she hissed in a voice that promised a much more agonizing and comprehensive castigation in the morning.

Leaning over she turned off the pillow speakers. The beds built in sleep aid had automatically switched on in response to Wayne's restless fidgeting. The woman's soothing, hypnotic voice fell silent. Gale went back to sleep.

Gingerly placing the umbrella by his side of the bed, Wayne slid quietly onto the dynamically tensioned and memory contoured mattress. He would not be hearing the last of this.

Tell the Birds

Jenny Tunstall

This morning our blackbird sang,
High in the horse chestnut
Outside our window.
Its song pierced through the glass
And, for a moment, touched me with the familiarity
of its joy.
I heard him take breath to comment
And looked up,
To greet his cynical, laughing words
With a smile.
But my smile was frozen in an instant
By the emptiness
Of his chair.
And then the sunshine felt cold
And grief raged within me
Keening to deny our loss.
My mind and senses are numbed,
For the world is still and strange
Despite the birds
Whose dispassionate songs of joy
Refuse to recognise the fact
That everything is changed.
His empty chair and empty desk,
Warmed now only by the sun,
Are the new normality.
Why then, in this awful, alien world
Of hushed humour
And carefully chosen words,
Has no-one, out of pity,
Remembered to tell the birds?

Circle of Pebbles

Patricia Lloyd

Rebecca pushed open the door with her shoulder as she lifted her suitcase and bag into the hallway of her apartment. After depositing the luggage in her bedroom she closed the front door and walked into the lounge.

How did she feel being home again? She would really have to stop talking to herself in the voice of the counsellor. It had been six months since she left here and voluntarily admitted herself to psychiatric care.

One part of her was glad to be back. This was home after all. She was able to accept now, that she was alone. That her small family had died and only she still lived. Talking about the deaths of her parents and brother had in part helped her to let go of them and move into her future. Frightening though isn't it, she thought?

She liked the way the rooms in her home, led off the hall. Walking into the super-modern kitchen she opened the fridge and saw that Mrs White had stocked it with food. Would she be in tomorrow to clean as usual? Tomorrow was Monday, wasn't it?

Pouring herself a glass of water she carried it into her bedroom. Everything looked the same. Pristine, clean and ordered. That was how she coped before, by keeping everything in order. Anything untoward threw her into panic and depression.

Mrs White had been wonderful. It had been she who had picked up on her erratic behaviour and asked the GP to visit.

A therapist said, 'It's how we see things that matters. Sometimes we don't see what is really there – we inflict on things what is in our minds – what is troubling us - a bit like the glass half full/half empty syndrome'.

Well, Rebecca was 'seeing' her flat for the first time for years. It is home, she thought, but it's cold, too tidy and stand-offish.

Tomorrow I'll buy that rocking chair I've always wanted and a bright red rug which will go with nothing in this room but will give colour and warmth to it.

She wandered into her study. Here the shelves were neatly stacked with files, books, and photo-albums. There were few ornaments. Before, she had avoided having things that were not 'useful'. She couldn't see the point. Now she did. Tomorrow she would buy flowers – a small posy for in here and a bouquet for the lounge, she thought.

As she turned to walk back into the hall, something caught her eye. She looked towards her desk. On it, in a neat circle, were one, two three......nine pebbles. Who put those there she thought? For a second – just a second, she panicked. Was she seeing something that wasn't there?

She walked over to the desk and picked up the largest pebble. It was fat and black and round. All the other pebbles were triangular.

So many triangles of pebble she noted...
One is dominant – it leads the circle – heavy and black. Others are grey.

The therapist had said, 'Don't be frightened to follow your thoughts wherever they lead.' Is the message here that there is a black leader in my life? Do I dance too much with grey?

Who put the pebbles there? Was it me? Dare I follow my thoughts?

Rebecca sat in the chair staring at the pebbles. Think positive. Look again. What do I see?

The black pebble is the leader of the circle. Leading the circle in a dance. Beige is dancing with brown and grey with white. A country reel of perfect formation.

What is their significance? Looking again, she sees - a circle – like a wedding ring signifying never ending love. There is space between the pebbles, showing that love needs space to grow. All the stones are different – like people. All are different and differences should be respected.

Who put the pebbles there and why?

Rebecca was calmly and silently reflecting on the pebbles when she heard a key in the lock.

'Anyone home?' called a voice that Rebecca recognised as Mrs White.

'I'm here,' replied Rebecca 'in the study.'

'Hello dear – welcome home. Fancy a cup of tea? I see you've found the pebbles. I left them for you. They meant a lot to me.'

Rebecca, following her into the kitchen asked why they were so significant.

Mrs White, filling the kettle turned her head . 'Someone I loved gave them to me when I was sad,' she said. 'They arranged them in a circle on my coffee table. They've kept me company and you know, I've never felt lonely since. What they did was help me reflect on my situation and come up with some good ideas of how to handle things.'

'You must keep them', said Rebecca, 'it would be awful if you were to feel lonely again.'

'No dear, their work is done for me. One day when you are strong again, you'll meet someone in more need of them and you will pass them on. Not now, maybe not for some time, but one day when you are strong again. Lovely to have you home dear – fancy a biscuit with your cuppa?'

Placing a mug of hot tea in front of Rebecca, Mrs White said 'I bought you some red carnations dear for your lounge – I thought they would cheer it up a bit.'

Rebecca nodded, sat back in her chair and sighed deeply.

All would be well – it really would.

Beauty Returned

Barbara Calvert

When the telephone rang, Lorraine Martin had been engaged in an activity that always demanded her unwavering attention. 'Doing her eyes' was not part of Lorraine's normal routine but on that special day she had been demonstrating a dogged persistence to get it right. She had, metaphorically speaking, so as not to disturb the contours around her eyes, breathed a sigh of relief when Issy had yelled up the stairs,

'It's O.K. mum, I'll get it,' and, as Lorraine flicked one last wayward eyelash into place, Issy had appeared in the doorway. 'You'll never guess who that was!' Issy, the mistress of cool, had been unusually animated. 'It's Auntie Vicky! She's over here for a couple of days. Did you know she was coming? Why didn't you invite her to the party?' But Issy hadn't waited for a reply. 'Anyway I told her about the party and she's coming over! She said she'll get a taxi and she should be with us in an hour or so. Isn't that great! Hurry up mum! People will be coming soon,' and, with that, Issy had dashed downstairs, most likely stopping for a quick glance in the mirror and a tug at her ramrod straight, party-perfect hair.

Lorraine's attempts at glamour, always a challenge, were now totally knocked off track. Why hadn't they invited Vicky to the party? After all, as Issy's godmother she had surely qualified to be at her god-daughter's eighteenth birthday party; the family party. All those closest to Issy would be there; most of them knowing her from the day she'd been born. Lorraine knew the answers she would have given if pushed. They had had no idea that Vicky would be over here on the day; Vicky was such a busy person; Vicky led such a glamorous life. They never dreamt that Vicky would be able to fit a simple little family gathering into her hectic schedule. All true of course, but not *the* truth. The distance between the once inseparable Lorraine and Vicky had grown as wide as the Atlantic Ocean that now literally came between them.

55

Lorraine had broken the news to Rex when he came out of the shower but they'd had little time to decide how to handle the situation.

'It'll be OK,' he said. 'She'll be well diluted in the crowd. They'll all want to talk to her and you can just be yourself. She'll soon be heading back to New York. How would her super-glossy magazine survive without its super-glossy editor even for a few days? It'll be fine.'

Her husband had been reassuring, but then he had never really understood Lorraine's feelings about Vicky. The bitterness, from what she saw as her friend's betrayal had, over time, become diluted but the hurt remained and memories of accusations and retaliations had hovered around Lorraine's life like cold, grey shadows.

Rex had been right though, at the party there would be very little time to reminisce about the past, or fill in the details of the years spent apart. Some of it, of course, Lorraine had read about in the weekend supplements and she had, on one occasion, even seen her old friend on a television programme about the Paris fashion shows. What could more appropriately sum up the yawning divide between Lorraine and her one-time best friend?

The party had gone well; better than expected – but then Issy had positively glowed at the sight of the pile of presents showered on her by loving grandparents, aunts, uncles and family friends. One present, however, had been delayed. Vicky had taken Issy aside and between them they had arranged a date for later in the week, for a 'day in town'. Exams were over, she was now eighteen, and godmother Vicky had a very special gift planned for her 'stunningly gorgeous' god-daughter.

And that explained why, just a week after the party, Lorraine could be heard screaming at her husband.

'I don't believe it! How could she! Isn't that just what you'd expect from her! My daughter is *not* going to be a model. I can't believe it's happening all over again. Does she hate me or something?'

Shadows of the past had become all too real. Lorraine and Vicky; friends, flatmates and earnest young journalists; seekers of truth with a mission to make their mark on the world. But Vicky weakened and wavered and finally abandoned their noble causes; firstly accepting a job on a lifestyle magazine, that in Lorraine's eyes, set her firmly onto the path of triviality. When Vicky eventually became the celebrity editor of a high-class fashion magazine, the separation of the two friends was complete . And now, under the pretence of taking her god-daughter out for a special birthday gift, she had used her network of contacts to seduce Lorraine's undoubtedly beautiful daughter into her own shallow and superficial world.

Rex and Lorraine found themselves powerless to restrain Issy's enthusiasm or to counter Vicky's enticements. So this was how Issy Martin metamorphosed into Bella Martin and blossomed and bloomed to become super-model extraordinaire under the Svengali-like, eagle eyes of her godmother.

As for Rex and Lorraine, their daughter had all but vanished: her new name, her fame; her home just a series of anonymous hotel rooms around the world. They had been left with the feeling that she existed in spirit only; transformed into another ethereal shadow by her wicked god-mother. The reassurances of Victoria – 'No-one calls her Vicky, Mum!' – had done little to quell the sense that they had somehow lost their daughter, that she had been stolen from them; but worst of all, that she had become a willing captive in an alien world.

It was five years later when, one unexceptional Saturday morning, the bell rang at the home of Rex and Lorraine. The young and ruggedly handsome young man standing on their doorstep, motor-cycle helmet in hand, was about the same age as Issy, and Lorraine greeted him with a vague sense of recognition. Matt Prince had been a school friend of Issy's. Like her, he'd been travelling the world in the years since school; though his travelling met with far greater approval from Lorraine than did her own daughter's. Matt was looking for Issy.

'I've tried to contact her several times, but it just seems impossible to get through to her.'
Lorraine sympathised. Surrounded by personal assistants, the PR crowd, designers, agents and their 'people', it often seemed to her mother that Issy had indeed disappeared from view.
Matt was raising funds for an orphanage and school for street children he had worked with in India. He was arranging a fund-raising ball in town and wanted a 'name' to help boost ticket sales. As an old school friend, transformed into a star, he had hoped that Issy might agree to come along. He hadn't yet fixed a date for the ball and would fit in with any time Issy was at home and might be prepared to get involved.

Of course Lorraine would do what she could, though inwardly the confidence she once had in her daughter's good nature and generosity had dwindled to a fragile scrap. Philanthropy and benevolence were not words Lorraine associated with the world her daughter now inhabited.

But, however we might think differently, life is just as likely to present pleasant surprises as it is to deal crushing blows. Issy came home and went to Matt's charity ball. The two old friends even danced together. Issy was happy. Issy realised she had not been as happy as this for a long time.

She met with her agents; she talked to the PR crowd; she had dinner with Victoria and she told them all... enough was enough. She came home again. Matt visited often. Lorraine and Rex felt that they owed him much; he had brought their daughter back to them. In time they expect – well hope – that there could even be a wedding. They won't be inviting Vicky – god-mother or no god-mother – but it's very unlikely that she would want to come anyway. She might get to hear about it of course; but surely she wouldn't dare send a present this time?

Hurt

Patricia Welford

When I was little I was forever falling down
grazed knees and elbows, I looked a clown
With red patches everywhere from head to toe
I slipped, tumbled, slid wherever I tried to go.

To play with the boys was all that mattered
coming back with clothes all torn and tattered
mother banned dresses, experience taught her
trousers were best for her tom-boy daughter.

Oh how I wish that I was still carefree and fey
the scrapes and scratches were cuddled away
while enclosed within mother's loving arms
hurts never caused any lasting alarms.

Now I'm careful climbing the lonely stair
no one to cry as I descend, beware
if I fall there's no one to shout
'she's hurt,' for there's no one about.

Before Winter's Window

Alan Beckett

I looked out, excited,
a distant yearning
beyond the window
a sudden, joyous need
to know again, to
run through the flakes.
Heh! It's snowing,
I must find the lads!

Try the door,
it's open.
Dark corridor, no one there.
Coming gang.
Creep, soft slippered, snug.
The back way, the fun way,
in sheepskin shoes slithering
along the polished floor.

Bitter cold.
Bare branches spire.
Bare legs, hands, face
flushed from the old log fire.
Memories scattering, falling leaves
little berries of recognition,
adorning trees of confusion.
Why is no one coming out to play?

Run, shout
kick the snowing air.
Fall about
happy again, no care.
Old Jack Frost,
Captain Arthritis
lost, in the past.
At last, here come the others.

But the gentle whispers stop
flaking on my grey hair.
The snow turns to pain
They start shouting again.
Could it be my mates, Pete and Derek?
I stumble trying hard
to gather a snowball
but *they* don't want to play.

Dressing gown flapping,
dragged and slithering through the slush
back into the corridor, back into my room.
Something is wrong,
was that the dinner gong?
Locked in, memory fading,
I look out, shaking, a distant ache
sat before winter's window
now, almost forgotten.

Best Ever

Ann Merrin

'Best ever! Best ever! You must be joking! Do you know how long I've been a chocolate taster? Thirty years. Thirty years! And never have I tasted anything that was enhanced by the flavour of swede. Not even a roast dinner benefits from its flavour! Get out, get out! Take one week's leave. Reconsider whether the chocolate trade is the place for you. I'll see you at 9.30 on the 31st October, in my office – if you have something to offer me. If you have nothing, a letter of resignation will suffice. Good morning.'

'Um, yes sir. 31st October. I'll see you then. Um good morning, sir.'

One week. Jim walked slowly from the lab, shoulders slumped. He was twenty-six, full of great innovative ideas for enlivening the chocolate industry. And, so far, his ideas had been well received, particularly the carrot and ginger creams. Now he seemed to have hit a brick wall. He really thought the swede went well with the dark chocolate. Perhaps there was a secret ingredient that he hadn't thought of yet.

By the time he reached home his brain had scrambled umpteen combinations. Swede and elderberry; swede and chervil; swede and Pimms. He knew the swede could come into its own, it was just a case of finding the right enhancement. He would do it.

He had one week. Perhaps a few days with Grandma might inspire him.

Jim's Grandma lived in Cornwall – that county with a slow pace of life and a fast acting magic. That was the place to be. If he couldn't find an answer there, he never would. Swede and...

Grandma was always pleased to see him. Her home was small and comfortable; her kitchen hung with herbs. She sat him down to a fine dinner on the first evening and listened gently to his tale of woe.

'Now why swede Jim? What made you choose that vegetable?'

Jim looked puzzled. 'Well, I don't know really. You know how sometimes things just seem right. I think it was the colour and the sweetness.'

'But those aspects weren't enough on their own?'

'No. No, it needs something more. Something to make it sparkle, to make it zing! Do you know what I mean?'

'I think so. Will you do some experimenting while you're here?'

'If that's ok with you? I know I can work it out, but I've only been given a week so I really have to get straight down to it.'
Jim went to bed that evening with his brain still buzzing. Grandma went to bed that evening with a little smile.

The morning broke bright and blue, with a chill that freshened sights and smells. After breakfast Jim walked along the coast path; his thoughts beginning to narrow down the list of flavours he might experiment with. Swede and lemon balm; swede and lavender; swede and mint…

For four days Jim tested and tasted. Grandma pottered into and out of the kitchen; sometimes tasting; sometimes offering suggestions. Always with a little smile around her eyes while Jim's face became longer by the hour.

At last, on day six, Jim collapsed into a chair by the fire and said, 'I think I'll write out my resignation.'

'Jim, I'm surprised at you!'

'But I have to see Mr. Wainwright at 9.30 in the morning. I've tried everything I can think of.'

'So, have you tried the Cornish Camomile?'

'Cornish Camomile? Oh come on Gran, have you made that one up? I've never heard of it.'

'Never heard of it? Think back Jim. Remember the summer holidays – the ice-cream treats we used to have? What can you remember about those?'

'Oh god yes! Imagine whatever flavour you fancied on that day and Grandma would provide it! It always looked like vanilla ice-cream with green bits in it but it could taste like strawberry or caramel or chocolate. How did you do that?'

'Cornish Camomile my darling!'

'Why didn't you mention it before!'

'I was hoping you might recall it for yourself. But as the week wore on, well I could see you'd need some help. What did you say you wanted for your swede flavouring?'

'Well, a bit of sparkle and zing! Sounds silly now, but why don't we give it a try?'

The two returned to the kitchen and three hours later Jim said goodbye to his Grandma and headed for home. He slept well that night and was up in optimistic mood the following morning. Wait until Wainwright tasted this!

'Well done Jim! 9.30 on the dot. And what do you have for me – taster or resignation?'

'Taster sir.'

'And what is <u>this</u> flavour named?'

'I wondered if you might like to name it sir. What would you most love to taste in your chocolate?'

'Hmm. Probably something like a champagne truffle or a cocktail. Chocolate cocktails – now that might be a good one.'

'I think this is it sir.'

Mr. Wainwright looked slightly suspicious but took the proffered chocolate.

'Good god man – this is perfect! How did you do it? It's got sparkle; it's got zing. I like it son, I like it! What's it made with?'

'Thank you sir. It's made with sw..., er um, a special ingredient grown in Cornwall. Something I've known about since I was a boy.'

'Well, you're a credit to the trade Jim. We need to get this into production as soon as possible. I'll have the marketing people get on the job right away. Consider your position with this company secure for the foreseeable future my boy. I'll see you later. And thank god you got rid of that bloody swede!'

'Thank you sir.'

Jim left the room with a little smile around his eyes – the one he had inherited from his Grandma.

The Bridge

Maureen Nicholls

The morning had started well. Simon had taken the day off, a rare occurrence for her workaholic husband, who, despite his many promises to reduce his work load, continued to add to it and pooh-poohed her protests that they never saw him.

'There'll be plenty of time for family soon,' was his stock answer. 'We're young and I intend to retire young then we'll have all the time in the world together and you'll soon be fed up with the sight of me.'

Sophie's own father had been much the same but her mother had never seemed to mind. She'd packed her children off to boarding school and happily filled her days with endless committees, lunches and charitable projects; forming close friendships with a number of like minded women, all grass widows of ambitious men, for whom, good works and dalliance often went hand in hand. It was not what Sophie had wanted or hoped for in her own marriage.

'Well kids, what shall we do today?' Simon asked the twins. Freddy was busy scraping up the last of his coco pops but Portia threw down her spoon with a clatter and jumped up.

'The Zoo, Daddy, let's go to the Zoo,' she shouted.

Simon groaned. 'The last time I had a day off we went to the Zoo. Wouldn't you rather try somewhere else? What about you Freddy?' Simon ruffled his small son's hair. 'Do you want to go to the Zoo?'

Freddy's mouth was full but he shook his head vigorously and swallowed fast until he could speak. 'No,' he said. 'I want to look over the bridge.'

It was Sophie's turn to groan and Simon laughed.

'Talk about a busman's holiday,' he said. 'How about we do both, if that's what you really want?' He looked from one to the other as both shouted their approval. 'Ok, but first I have to make a few calls. Hurry up Freddy, you can't scrape any more from that dish and Portia, I refuse to take you wearing pyjamas so go and change. Both of you wash your hands and faces and don't forget to clean your teeth.'

Sophie cleared the table and stacked the dishwasher. There was no point in changing her clothes, the jeans and sweater she wore were perfectly adequate for what was planned. As she wiped her hands, the telephone rang and she waited, expecting Simon to pick it up but he was in the down stairs loo and shouted for her to take the call. She sighed and picked up the receiver but before she could say a word, the caller shouted down the phone.

'Simon, it's happening for God's sake come, quick,' he sounded desperate.

'I'm afraid Simon isn't available right now,' Sophie's tone was cool. 'This is his wife. Perhaps you are not aware that it's his day off? Please be kind enough to call back tomorrow.'

'For Christ's sake woman get Simon. It's the bridge…he's got to come, I need to speak to him now, get him, quick.'

'What bridge are you talking about?' Sophie was puzzled. Simon was a design engineer of some note, whose speciality was bridges. When they'd moved to Bristol, he'd been approached by the charity governing the Clifton Suspension Bridge and asked to join the Committee. He had of course jumped at the chance but it was merely an honorary position and had more to do with fund raising than engineering. As far as she knew, this was the only bridge he had dealings with right now.

'He must have told you about the problems we've been having, for God's sake, let me speak to him NOW,' the man yelled.

How rude! Sophie dropped the phone and ran for Simon. She watched his face as he took the call. His answers were cool and detached despite the shouting coming from the other end. He asked a number of questions she didn't understand, nodding at the responses given. Finally he paused, as though considering his course of action.

'Hmm,' he said eventually. 'I think you are worrying unnecessarily but I'll pop up and take a look.'

Simon turned and smiled at Sophie. 'Sorry darling, it's just Ted being over anxious. I won't be long, why don't you meet me at the bridge when the kids are ready and that way we can keep them both happy,' he touched her face. 'Don't look so worried, I assure you, there is nothing for you to worry about. Let me sort this out and then we can all go and have a nice lunch at the Zoo together.'

She watched him leave; leisurely, unhurried, seemingly relaxed. Unlike the man on the phone, Ted, or whatever his name was, who had sounded frantic, almost frightened. And what had he meant about the problems? What problems? Surely Simon would have told her had there been any serious problems? Wouldn't he? Oh come on Sophie, she told herself, when did he last share a problem with you?

Since the day they'd married, it was Simon's avowed intention that she be shielded from all the boring problems and pin pricks of life. He worked hard to provide her with every comfort and protect her from all harm. He dealt with all the financial matters, chose houses, schools, holidays and even domestic help. In return, he asked only that she love him, be a gracious hostess and a beautifully dressed partner whom he could proudly escort into society. It was also a matter of great pride to him that she had managed to produce the requisite number of children – two, in one go; an excellent solution to the tiresome nine months out of the loop business. So, what did that make her? A mindless WAG with an atrophied brain or simply a rather lazy, kept woman. How the hell had she allowed it to happen. She adored Simon but he was becoming more and more like a benign dictator rather than a passionate, sharing husband. Things must change and if he was so good at building bridges, he'd better start with a much needed one to cross the chasm fast developing in their marriage.

Freddy and Portia were ready to go. In his favourite combat hoody, Freddy was saved from looking like a mini ASBO hooligan by the small teddy bear tucked into his front pocket. Portia however, was a vision in bright pink from head to toe and carried a little pink shiny handbag on her arm. The colour did nothing to tone down her bright ginger curls and 'Barbie wears Prada' was the thought uppermost in Sophie's head when she looked at her little daughter.

It was a short walk to the Bridge from their house on Sion Hill. As they rounded the corner at the top and looked across to Brunel's masterpiece, proudly spanning the Avon Gorge, they could see cars backed up as far as the end of the slip road and continuing down the Promenade, creating total gridlock. As they drew nearer, Simon could be seen in the centre of a small huddle of men. Tall, calm, one might almost say, aloof, despite the obvious agitation of the others around him. He seemed totally oblivious to the angry tooting and shouting from the waiting drivers.

The stream of invective pouring from the open car windows as she walked past them, made Sophie want to block her children's ears. Holding their hands tightly, she hesitated behind the group surrounding Simon, uncertain whether to approach him. She was about to return home when Freddy, tugging at her hand, pulled her towards the path for pedestrians. Sophie's resistance gave way in the face of Freddy's all consuming passion. His most favourite thing in the whole world was to get to the middle of the bridge and peer down at the river, some 300 feet below. Sophie didn't share her small son's love of heights but at least they would be away from the rumpus and all the foul language. Why was it she wondered, that men always swore and shouted whenever something went wrong. The women stood silent, if grumpy but the men were ready to go to war.

She heard someone yelling. It sounded like 'lady come back, come back,' but assuming it was nothing to do with her, she continued without check until they reached the centre of the bridge. Here, all was quiet and calm. The toll barriers remained down at both ends, preventing cars from crossing and she and the children were the only pedestrians on the bridge. Sophie hated heights, unlike her son who had already climbed up onto the guard rail and, given half a chance, would have climbed higher if she hadn't restrained his enthusiasm.

Portia, uninterested in doing the same was looking back towards the rumpus surrounding her Daddy.

'Why are those men shouting at us?' she asked.

Sophie was busy steadying Freddy and didn't look round.

'They're not shouting at us darling,' she said. It's the car drivers who are being held up for some reason. I expect the toll machine is broken again. The barrier won't go up when the machine breaks down. Freddy, for goodness sake, stop trying to climb higher or I'll make you get down,' she hung onto the back of his hoody before turning to look at her daughter.

'I think they are shouting at us Mummy,' Portia said, pointing to a small group of men who seemed to be glued to the bridge supports but were facing them and gesticulating frantically.

'Oh dear, I think you're right, they do want us to go back,' Sophie said. We'd better do as they say. Get down Freddy, we'll try to come back later.' Still holding the back of his hoody, she gave a quick tug and Freddy reluctantly climbed down. 'Stop moaning poppet, I promise we'll come back, hold my hand and be a good boy.'

They had taken just a few steps when the ground beneath their feet seemed to shudder and a terrible, metallic whine filled the air, hurting their ears and setting their teeth on edge. Sophie couldn't see what was causing the noise until, looking up, she saw one of the huge steel girders of the bridge support, rising slowly, inexorably, skywards. The cries of the waiting men reached her.

'RUN,' they were shouting. But she couldn't move. Fear held her feet to the ground as firmly as rivets.

Terrified, she became aware of Simon running towards her and her breathing quickened. Simon was coming, Simon would save them, SIMON…she was shouting but no sound came.

The screaming metallic whine increased and she wanted to block her ears but the children were clinging to her hands and her legs. She couldn't move and the pain in her ears became unbearable. The bridge began to move and with a sudden horrific crash, the whining stopped and for a moment all was quiet. Beneath her feet, Sophie felt the floor start to rise up into the air; soon they were flat to the surface but slipping back and slipping down. Another loud crack screamed out and the middle span of the bridge broke in several places until it resembled a massive letter W.

Simon's face appeared above her, yelling for them to hang on. The children were clamped desperately to Sophie's legs but they were all sliding towards the chasm which had opened up behind them. With a desperate effort, Simon reached one of Sophie's hands and pulled until she could feel the bone leave its socket. Screaming with pain, she stretched up with her other hand, frantically feeling for something to hold, something to help bear the weight but every surface was jagged and sharp, the edges cut into her skin like serrated knives. She felt faint and fought to stay conscious, aware of the steady traction caused by the children's grip on her legs and waist. A strange hand grabbed hers and another grabbed the back of her jacket, she was being hauled up and the children clung to her like limpets, digging their feet into the shattered tarmac to support their hold.

At the top of the broken and now vertical section of roadway, she was being lifted up and out, away from the surface in order to get her over the gap but this left the children without any support for their feet, they were left dangling from Sophie's legs. She felt the sudden and drastic change in their hold and heard their screams. She started to shout 'STOP! THE CHILDREN ARE FALLING, STOP, STOP....' Her legs were suddenly free; the weight of the children was gone. She fought the hands above her, screaming and scrabbling at her legs but deaf to her screams, they continued to lift her until she could no longer remain conscious and allowed the merciful blackness to descend.

Sophie walked slowly towards the river, as she did everyday the hospital allowed, with a minder from the hospital at a respectful but close distance. The tide was out and in the pale wintry sun, the banks of billowing mud lay exposed and glistening, like enormous cushions of rat coloured marshmallows. Gaunt and hollow eyed, she scanned the banks, searching for a sign, any sign; a shoe, a sock, a little pink bag, a teddy bear but there was nothing. A multitude of secrets lay hidden, held fast in the obscene glutinous depths, secrets known only to the tide.

Above her, stark against the sky, were the remnants of the broken bridge. But Sophie never looked up. She hated this place but was drawn inescapably to where, in her minds eye, she relived the horror of watching her children fall and being sucked into oblivion. Unable to help them, unable to be with them because Simon in saving her, had allowed them to fall.

She heard Simon's voice calling behind her. She had refused to see him, refused to listen to anything he had to say and now he had followed her, to this private hell, how dare he! She ignored him and was about to walk on when she heard the children's voices calling 'Mummy'. Turning she saw Portia and Freddy holding Simon's hands. They hesitated for a moment before breaking away from their Daddy and running towards her. Both children threw themselves at her, attaching themselves like limpets to any part of her they could reach with their small bodies and hands.

Sophie couldn't speak. She had believed them to be dead. She had believed it so firmly and would not listen to anyone who tried to tell her otherwise, not even the Doctors in the hospital. Day and night, for many weeks, she had screamed in terror, calmed only by the oblivion inducing drugs.

She touched each child, afraid she would feel nothing, afraid this was one more horror to add to the list of horrors. But their little bodies were real, solid, warm. They wriggled and squirmed closer, trying to get beneath her skin if it were possible.

She fell to her knees and wrapped her arms around them, unable to make a sound, her tears falling silently.

'Sophie?' Simon was on his knees beside them.

She looked at her husband's changed face. The calm arrogance was gone, the smooth assurance had given way to hesitant need and the tears followed furrows and lines she had never seen before on his handsome face.

'Simon.' Still holding her children, she held out her arm and embraced him into the circle, feeling the unity and safety of their small quartet like a blanket. The terror and pain of the past weeks beginning at last, to recede.

The Park

Jane Mason

Remember when I pushed you on the swing
The sound of childish laughter filled the air
I felt the satisfaction of Motherhood
And I was fulfilled

The sound of childish laughter filled the air
As I pushed you on the zip slide
And I was fulfilled
You were now at school

As I pushed you on the zip slide
Your brother waited patiently in his pram
You were now at school
I had time to lavish on another

Your brother waited patiently in his pram
I felt the satisfaction of Motherhood
I had time to lavish on another
Remember when I pushed you on the swing

The Right Choice

Patricia Welford

Emma was in the kitchen preparing a salad for lunch when she heard Gregg's key in the lock. He'd been out all the previous night. She took off her apron, smoothed down her dress and hurried out into the hall, anxious to gauge his mood. Gregg came in, his eyes clouded with drink or worse.

'What are you doing littering up the hall. Get into the bedroom where you belong.' Emma turned, her heart sinking as she walked into the bedroom, desolate; he couldn't be in a worse state. He followed and pushed her roughly.

'Well, what are you waiting for, get undressed.' Obediently she stripped down to her underwear leaving her high heels on, hoping that her subservience would protect her from the worst of his violence.

Gregg was too far gone to do anything but look, knowing this, enflamed his anger further, as he stared at her standing there in her underwear. Raking his eyes over the midnight blue basque, matching thong and black stockings held up by suspenders, realising she was wearing just what he liked best, frustration made his rage bubble over.

'Look at you! you whore!' he shouted, grabbing her brutally by the arm. 'Dressed up to seduce, you little slut.' Open palmed he slapped her face so hard she stumbled backwards into the bathroom door frame, hitting the back of her head as she went down, seeing nothing but a red mist before she passed out.

Later Emma sat up from her sprawled position on the bathroom floor, her head ached, woozy from Gregg's blow. As she put her hand up she could feel a large swelling where her head had hit the doorframe. She looked around half-dazed at the pristine white bath, toilet and washbasin, the spotless tiled floor. Fresh towels hung neatly in their places, soaps and creams dutifully lined up. Everything normal like any other well-kept bathroom, the only difference being the bolt on the outside of the door, not inside as expected in most households.

Getting up, her legs stiff and wooden, she staggered across to the mirror. There she saw that her left eye and cheek were bruised by Gregg's slap. She moved over to the door and tried it. Of course she was locked in again.

'Gregg, let me out. I'm sorry,' she begged, calling through the door, 'Gregg please, tell me what to do, tell me what I've done wrong?'

Nothing but silence greeted her. Gregg must have gone out again. The light from the window proved the day was darkening. It would be about five o'clock she guessed and night was clearly on its way. She must have been out for some time, at least four hours.

Desperate thoughts winged in chaotic confusion around her mind. The cold from the floor had penetrated her bones while she had lain on them. Emma had never felt so afraid, the anger and violence from Gregg was escalating. *What if he killed me next time,* she thought, *and there would be a next time of that there was no doubt. She couldn't stay, she had to get out, escape from Gregg she must. But how? The window, she must get out of the window, but it's very small, her clearer mind argued, I've got to try, her desperation stressed.*

Opening the window she looked out. She was on the first floor. If she could squeeze herself out somehow maybe she could reach the lilac tree. Would it be strong enough? She doubted it would have many footholds for climbing down, but it would definitely break her fall.

'Oh God,' Emma whined. 'I can't do it,' she sat down putting her head on to her knees. She wept, thinking, *I will die here bruised and battered into submission, an imprisoned pleasure machine that's all I am, a toy to be broken at will.*

But part of the old Emma reared up in her consciousness. Emma the keen gymnast who existed before Gregg, before she fell in love with the handsome man who had charmed her into this disastrous marriage. Emma stiffened her resolve, stood up again and returned to look out of the window. It was now completely dark. The bathroom was at the back of the house and faced towards the cliffs and the sea below. The house itself fronted the road to Coombe Deep, half a mile away, but was set well back and isolated enough to be out of any street lighting.

A cold offshore wind blew in her face, a reminder that she was scantily dressed and vulnerable to the November weather. Backing away from the window, she faced facts. *Could she get out of the window, into the tree and survive the cold. Only one way to find out she resolved, one step at a time. If I can't get out of the window everything else is impossible.*

Taking up all the towels, she threw them out towards the lilac. Two missed but one caught high up and she decided to leap for the top of the tree hoping that the towel would cushion her from the worst of the branches. After throwing out her shoes, she stood on the toilet seat and pushed her head out twisting sideways until her left shoulder was outside. Pressing down she eased her right shoulder through and moving forward with care she managed to get herself out as far as her waist. Now she had to stop and reassess. She could turn now and shuffle out in a sitting position holding on to the lintel above the window, but would she have enough purchase to stand and then turn round? Would it be better to stay as she was and somehow dive out headfirst? Working out in her mind however, if she was unable to push outwards with her legs, she'd almost certainly miss the tree, falling straight down to the ground.

Shuddering at the thought, Emma decided to turn. With gritted teeth and biting her lip with concentration, she twisted on to her back and inched further out using her hands to pull her body upwards. Reaching for the lintel she grabbed hold, leant forward and up pressing down with her hands. She balanced her weight on her forearms and then eased her legs fully out, feeling for the sill with her feet. At last, she was now standing on the sill. She let out a sigh of relief, first part accomplished.

Turning slowly round again so her back leaned against the window frame and wall, Emma eased to one side for the bathroom light to illuminate the lilac tree more clearly. It was just too far to step into but if she angled her jump up and out, she hoped she would be able to leap across and grab at one of the main branches without falling into the tree mass. Using the towels as a marker, she took a deep breath, and launched herself out.

'Yes!' Emma felt a moment of triumph as her old gymnastic skills propelled her to the right branch. Her hands grabbed and held, but her momentum still swung her body into the tree partially covered by the towel but some of the surrounding branches still pierced her skin in numerous places, fortunately just missing her face and neck. Then her feet steadied on a lower branch. She hugged the tree exhausted, scratched, and bleeding, but elated that she had made it.

Climbing down, she began to look for her shoes but at ground level, the bathroom light was insufficient. She couldn't find them. Concluding that the height of the heels would not be any help, Emma rescued the two towels from the grass. Wrapping one around her waist and the other round her shoulders, she moved down the path towards the front of the house. As she did so, a car door slammed. Gregg's voice shouted across the darkness.

'Thanks for the company Ian. I'll see you tomorrow.'

Emma shrank back, now she was in real trouble. Gregg would know she was out before she had even left the garden. Turning in a panic she fled, down the back garden, the towel spinning away from her shoulders, she sped away from the road towards the cliff path. Her feet hardened by years of gymnastics took the ground fairly well but the stones still bit into her soles, the cuts hardly noticed as the panic and adrenalin pushed her onwards. Gaining the cliff path she had to slow, in the menacing dark she imagined all the horrors of falling down to the sea below.

Unfortunately for Emma, Gregg went immediately upstairs to check on her and although she had gained the cliff path, the dropped towel indicated which way she had gone.

'So it's a game of cat and mouse.' Gregg laughed aloud. He rushed back downstairs and started to follow. On reaching the cliff path he surmised that Emma would go towards the town. He confidently turned to his left striding out, blown up with the lust of the chase, hungry for revenge, reckless with alcohol consumed earlier with his mates.

Emma meanwhile, pressed on picking her way, nervous with dread, feeling the cliff on her right blindly following where her fingertips led. The path was narrow with loose stones, sharp rocks under her feet, her stockings already in shreds. Her towel kept slipping so she had to hold it against her body with her left hand and so she progressed. The cold numbed her as she stubbornly crept on.

'I know this path' she mumbled, 'I know this path' she repeated to herself again and again, summoning up courage. To keep herself alert she repeated a mantra in her head. *I won't fall if I keep away from the edge its wide enough as long as I keep my hand on the cliff wall I can do it.* All thought of Greg following seemed insignificant to the fear of falling. She knew she would hear him. There was no sound, no sound at all but for the distant drum of the waves beckoning her to step toward them. *If I hear him she whimpered to herself, I'll fight for my life, one of us will be over that edge.*

The cruel wind continued to buffet her body, but grim determination kept her going. Almost delirious now, thoughts tumbling together. *Feel the cliff wall, feel the wall. Keep going, keep going. I won't fall if I keep away from the edge its wide enough as long as I keep my hand on the cliff wall I can do it.* Her head thumped with dull pain and she could sense that her eye was almost closed with swelling.

Bravely she struggled on, repeating her mantra, towards the headland and the lighthouse at Coombe Gate, which lay one mile on. There was a bike shelter there, she remembered, where she could rest away from the wind. Then she could take the road into the village, where she hoped to get to the Anchor pub before it closed.

'Left, right,' Emma slurred. 'Listen to my fingers, keep going, keep going.' Everything became a nightmare, her body numbed with cold her hesitant steps replicating the rhythm of her mantra, her fingers leading the way until she was so exhausted and terrified she doubted she would ever reach the lighthouse. Then there it was at last, its beam lighting up the sky as it swept over the sea. Safety for the Ships out in the Coombe Bay and safety for Emma if she could just keep going. Digging deep within herself with one huge effort, she staggered forward to the welcoming light. Eventually completely spent she arrived and collapsed into the shelter against the lighthouse base.

Nurse Beth Sanders looked down at the bruised and battered girl on the bed suffering from concussion and exposure.

'Look at the huge bruise on her cheek bone and eye Jed. That's recent, along with the bleeding feet and scratches, but see these older ones, here on her side and that one right across her stomach, she's been systematically beaten. She must have desperate the poor lamb, but how did she get to the lighthouse? Dressed like that with next to nothing on? Do you think she had been dumped there? Lucky you found her Jed, she wouldn't have lasted the night that's for sure.'

'Well the dog found her not me, good job we walked to the lighthouse tonight; we sometimes go the other way. I reckon she's run off and come by the cliff path. I'd have seen her before, if she had come by the town road. Look I think she's coming round.'

Emma could hear a voice from far away

'Hi there, are you awake?' a kind voice echoed. 'Come on open your eyes for me, there's a good girl'

Emma struggled through a haze of half memory back to consciousness for the second time that day. Groaning as she woke, every part of her body hurting, she opened her eyes, turning her head to see a nurse bending over her.

'You're in hospital love and safe now.'

Sitting up panic stricken, Emma stuttered, 'He mustn't find me you mustn't let him know where I am.'

'Now, now love, don't worry, Jed brought you here. You were at the bottom of the lighthouse do you remember why?'

Emma looked over to where a tall fair haired man in his thirties stood hovering by the door. 'Please don't tell him you found me', she pleaded.

'Anyone trying to hurt you will have to get past me first.' Jed growled. 'Lovely lass like you stranded in next to nothing, feet, and body torn and battered, he deserves to hang.'

'We can find you a safe place, a women's refuge, don't you fret.' Beth reassured. 'You have a nasty bump on the back of your head. Can you remember your name?'

'It's Emma, Emma Heinon.'

'You could press charges you know, the police will want to interview you, we had to inform them. I told them not to come until tomorrow morning.'

'I don't know what to do. I can't think.'

'Well that's for you and the police to decide love. Come on Jed it's time to let Emma rest.'

Emma watched them both go out of the door, realising she hadn't thanked Jed for rescuing her. She fell asleep almost immediately, musing that she hoped to see him again to thank him.

When she woke in the morning, she felt much better and to the nurse's satisfaction ate her breakfast with gusto. At 10 am the door opened and a police sergeant came in and approached her bed. Bringing the bedside chair closer he sat down and introduced himself.

'Good morning I'm Sergeant Phillip Grover.' He smiled and shook her hand. 'I'm here to take a statement about what happened yesterday.'

'I'm not sure whether I want to make any charges. I just want to find a safe place where I can think things through for a while before I decide. Gregg is not a bad man, but he has a problem with drink and drugs.'

Phillip Grover leant over and took her hands in his, 'Gregg Heinon was found dead at the bottom of Gull cliff this morning at six am by a fisherman. He noticed the body while going out to his lobster pots. Nothing to be done I'm afraid. It looks as if he missed his footing. Do you know what he would be doing out on the cliff last night?'

Emma looked at him her hand up to her mouth with shock, tears filling her eyes. Hardly able to speak she stammered. 'He was chasing me, I'd escaped through the bathroom window but I went towards the lighthouse, my only chance of him not catching me was to go away from the town.'

'Well we'll have to await the post mortem, but by the looks of you and what I've heard of his habits, it's most likely the cause of death will be accidental. You can go home when you're fit and well.' He smiled at her kindly, still holding her hands he squeezed them firmly. 'Sometimes fate takes a hand in people's lives. Go home and start your life again, you deserve it. He gave her hands one last squeeze then got up and left.

Alone again, for the first time in a long time she felt calm and unafraid. Whatever difficulties lay ahead she felt confident and free to restart her life. *Perhaps*, she thought sleepily, *that new career as a fitness trainer I once dreamed about*. Then with the sedatives once more claiming her consciousness, Emma fell asleep.

Accidental Damage

Jenny Tunstall

The insurance company wrote today. I shall be staying with my sister and wearing my Oxfam clothes for a while longer. Insurance. I used to insure everything; the car, our holidays, the washing machine and tumble-dryer. Everything, really. Just to be on the safe side. Pity they don't sell you insurance against marital infidelity. When you think of his flabby face and his great, bulging stomach, you wouldn't think the premium would have been all that high.

I worked it out straight away. The sudden interest in business trips did seem strange, but that wasn't it. No, what gave it away was that he suddenly wanted me to do new things in bed. After twenty three years we'd let it all get rather routine, like cleaning your teeth and checking that you'd locked the front door, but it was civilised and comfortable. And then he suddenly had a whole lot of new ideas. I suppose they could have been from a book, but he wasn't at all hesitant like you'd think he would have been. He knew what to do. He'd obviously already tried it. I knew then, but of course I had no proof.

I thought I had everything worked out until then; you know, life, the world and what my role was. I was his wife, first and foremost. The one and only. The one who did his washing, cooked his meals, kept his house, insured his belongings and satisfied his physical needs. I was certain he needed me. Perhaps I was a bit smug about it. I went to my Women's Guild meetings and enjoyed my library books and the odd matinee at the cinema and I treated myself to a trip over to the big shops in Harrogate every so often and I thought all that was mine by rights. I was confident; self-satisfied, I suppose. But after I realised that he was, well, not behaving, I wasn't so sure of myself. You see I wasn't the one and only any more. Doubt crept in. Somehow everything I'd thought I controlled slipped a little away from me. I even let some insurance policies lapse. And when he touched me I just wanted to cry and say 'it's not fair'; like a kid.

And then I got my proof. He was away on one of his 'business' trips and I decided to turn out his socks and pants drawer. At the bottom of the drawer was a carrier bag and inside the bag was a book. I dropped it as though it was red hot. There was a scribbled note sticking out from between the pages. 'Here's what you ordered, you naughty boy,' it said. The book was called Taming your Partner's Passion: a guide for older men with younger sexual partners. Well, I knew it wasn't my passion he wanted to tame. I'm a year older than him.

Once the first shock had worn off, I saw red. I went completely mad. I tore that filthy book up, page by page and I put all the bits in the dustbin. But that wasn't enough; I just got angrier and angrier. I'd never known rage like it: almost like my sister, though hers is because of the Change. I knew I'd really lost control when I grabbed one of those nice coloured glass vases we brought back from Malta. I threw it as hard as I could and it hit my parents in their Golden Wedding frame. They smashed all over the place and I'd only just missed his Auntie Ivy's antique chiming clock that we hadn't insured. That sobered me up. But then I just started crying. It was awful.

I didn't sleep that night. I kept trying, but my mind just wouldn't stop. I lay there, staring up at the artex swirls, with my tears making the hair at my temples sticky. But by morning I knew what I had to do. I had to scare him; really scare him. I'd leave him; just for a week or two. Just long enough for him to run out of clean socks and get fed-up with heated-up pies. I'd stay with my sister. Then he'd have to beg me to come home and I'd be able to make my demands. But first I had to show him just how angry I was. A confrontation. A good raising of my voice. He'd be home the next day, so that gave me a day to get organised. I packed my little suitcase, ready. Just a few clothes, my newest underwear and my jewellery. And then I took myself shopping to calm down.

I stayed out most of the day and when I got home I knew he'd been there. I put my carrier bags down on the kitchen table and listened for him. I could feel myself shaking. I was ready though; ready for my angry speech and dramatic exit. But let him come in search of me. I waited ages. Eventually I went through to the lounge to see if he was there. He wasn't, but there was a piece of paper propped against the clock. I read it. It was from him. Our marriage had stopped working years ago, he said; it was best for both of us to make a fresh start, he said; he was going to be courageous and make the break, he said; he'd be in touch about collecting his clothes and model-making stuff and everything. That fat bastard had gone; just gone without even letting me scream at him. Courage! Oh yes, it takes a lot of courage to sneak in and leave a pathetic note. And I was expected just to accept it quietly.

If I'd gone mad the day before, I went bezerk now. I didn't really know who I was maddest with; him for being such a bastard or me for being so easily fooled. I felt like something had smashed all my happy years, so that even the memories were no good. Our wedding photo went first. Then his model Spitfire: that crunched beautifully under foot. Then the best china, plate by plate. And then his Auntie Ivy's antique chiming clock. Uninsured. But the more I smashed the madder I got. Now here's a strange thing about utter rage: you reach a point of total madness, but total calm. It came to me in a flash. Seemed perfect. Seemed to hurt him without hurting me. Very strange. I'd been making some new curtains for the back bedroom. They were lying next to the gas fire. So I spread them out a bit and fed a corner or two into the fire. And then switched it on.

The horror knocked some sense into me. Flames whoofed up and shot across the fabric. I was lucky my own clothes didn't catch. And the roar of those flames! I fled into the hallway and my lungs were heaving with all the smoke. I did wonder why the smoke detector hadn't gone off. I remember seeing the battery compartment open and empty. That will affect the insurance claim, I thought; but that fire was after me and I was through the kitchen and out the back door as fast as I could. When Carol at number thirty opened her door to me, all I could say was 'fire!'.

The firemen were really sweet to me. And the Police. I told them it was an accident, of course. The house was gutted. It wasn't until I was inside Carol's that I remembered my little suitcase and all my new knickers. Too late. So here I am at my sister's, trying to keep clear of her rages and trying not to think about who has worn these Oxfam clothes before me. I've thought of another insurance I should have had: loss of occupation. I won't be his wife much longer. No more big shops for me. And God only knows where I'll live. They don't sell insurance for smugness and confidence and self-satisfaction. Or insurance against temporary loss of sanity. Maybe I should have kept that book after all and got myself a toy-boy to tame.

The Other Half

Maureen Nicholls

So happy to meet you
Now have I this clear,
You have four children?
Are they all here?
Wonderful!
Mine of course are all at school,
Boarding you know.
I weep tears
Whenever they go, but then
So pleasant to be on one's own again
Don't you agree?
How silly, of course…
Yours come home to take tea,
…everyday!
Do tell,
How does one manage with the children about?
Does Nanny come running whenever they shout?
No?
No Nanny?
One jokes!
One does not?
Oh! I see.
How terribly, frightfully..
Brave…
Goodness me!

White War

Jane Mason

Upon the time marked table, it languished unopened. Kitty had already guessed the contents; staggered someone could be so remarkably generous, in these treacherous times of make do and mend.

Perhaps some mysterious well-wisher had heard of her plight and decided to assist.

Maybe one of those black marketeers had acquired the parcel, for which he had no market. Whatever the reason she sincerely thanked her champion for helping to realise a dream.

Chipping her cigarette in the ashtray, to save for later, the parcel eased its way on to her lap. Excited butterflies rose up in her stomach, in anticipation of this joy-filled moment, as she prised apart the folds, until the contents were laid open.

The startlingly white material revealed itself, shining with the unmistakable lustre of silk. Not one single day had passed, since June 1941, when she hadn't agonised over how she was going to fulfil her wish now. She imagined herself as Veronica Lake, starring in a floor length gown. Men would be bowled over and women glaringly envious.

How would Frank react, when he gazed adoringly at her in this extravagant dress?

Would he recognise her? It was amazing how word had meandered its way around town, whispering her plight from ear to ear. Fifteen coupons had been beyond her means, to purchase the Home Stores basic dress, let alone this luxurious article.

Kitty caressed the material over and over hardly believing her luck. The relinquished tissue paper scattered mutinously from the sumptuous folds of material and she lovingly held the dress against her shoulders, as the hem skirted the linoleum flooring of the kitchen. It would need to be altered slightly. The previous owner had been taller than her. She was yearning to try the garment on, plucking nervously at her unsightly overalls in agitation.

Alone in the bedroom she removed her scarf, allowing lustrous auburn locks to cascade appealingly about her shoulders. Unbuttoning the boiler suit she hurriedly thrust this away from her, eager to try on the frock. In her haste she forgot to remove the clumsy work boots. Laughing quietly, hugging this dizzy secret to herself, she slid the dress over her head and smoothed the material against her slim waist and curvaceous hips. Turning to gaze into the full length mirror the image glittering in its depths was of a sexy screen siren.

She swished her hips snakelike side to side and avidly watched the rippling effect of the silky material, swaying with the movement. Thanks to the length of the dress she wasn't going to need to purchase new shoes or stockings. Her legs would be fully covered.

Lifting her hair out, away from her neck, she toyed with the idea of whether to have it in an up do. She was certainly going to ensure it was fully dressed and showed her face off to its best advantage. She was going to be a swan, casting aside her ugly duckling work attire and emerging triumphant from factory life.

Her eager need to witness her appearance in the dress satisfied, she gently pulled the material back over her head and hunted in the wardrobe for a suitable hanger. Kitty hung the dress above her wardrobe door and lay back on the bed entranced, marvelling at this wonderful masterpiece entering her life so suddenly and astonishingly.

It was only then with a pang she realised. Someone else had worn it. How could they part with such a wonderful reminder? It didn't look as though it had ever been worn before. Why had someone purchased such a dress and never worn it? How curious. Was it pain that had made them part with it or gladness to allow someone else to use it in these days of uncertainty. She would never know. The dress seemed all the more enigmatic to Kitty.

A hard tap at the door broke into her intimate moment. Sighing happily she unfolded herself from the bed to answer it. Pulling the door open her heart flew into her mouth.

Her bubble burst like dirty water down a drainpipe.

'Telegram for you miss', trilled the boy, handing her the piece of paper with her name and address neatly typed on the front.

Back in the bedroom Kitty carefully propped the message in front of her dressing table mirror. Why now? It wasn't fair. All that longing and hoping. To have it snatched away in a foul knock on the front door.   She'd open it later and carry on dreaming for a bit longer. Maybe this dress was only meant to be longingly admired, not worn.   She would give anything now, to have him here in this room with her, to gaze in wonder at the dress and appreciate its sentiment.

Realisation dawned as a scream began in the back of her throat and forced its dark stealthy way into her mouth, combining menacingly with the air raid siren.   Frank, her brother, wouldn't be there to give her away.

The Applicant

Patricia Lloyd

Rising from her desk, Janet Maclean opened the interview room door to show out the last but one applicant.

'Thank you for coming Mrs Anstee. My colleagues and I will be reviewing all the interviews this afternoon and one of us will contact you tomorrow morning to let you know the outcome. Can you find your way out? Good. We'll be in touch tomorrow. Goodbye.'

It had been Janet who had suggested that rather than discuss each individual applicant after their interview, they put aside time at the end of the day to go through each one then. Jane Morrisey and Philippa Granger were used to Janet 'taking control' and were quite happy to fall in line with her wishes because, in the end, she got to do most of the work.

Philippa was especially glad because she needed to be away on time that day, as she had a 30th birthday celebration that evening. She went to fetch the next applicant from the foyer. Bringing her into the room she introduced Jennifer Williams. Jennifer was a smart woman, someone who had the confidence to grow into her own style. She was slim, wearing smart jean trousers, a pink top and tan chukka boots and carrying a tan leather haversack. Jane, checking her application, was astonished to see that Jennifer was 46 years old; she thought she looked at least ten years younger.

Jennifer sat in the chair offered and Janet (as usual) opened the interview by explaining that the position was about providing care for older people. She explained that support workers needed to be willing to do shift work as well as working bank holidays on a rota basis.

Jane broke in with information about salary, holidays etc.

Not to be outdone, Philippa explained how the interview would be structured.

'Right Jennifer,' said Janet. 'Tell us what it is that led you to apply for this position.'

93

Jennifer, looking very calm and in control of the situation, replied. 'I've spent the last two years caring for my Aunt. She had cancer of the bowel which eventually spread to other parts of her body and six months ago she was told that she wouldn't recover. Before Auntie was ill, I lived away – in Liverpool and worked as a secretary with the NHS. When she became ill I moved in with her and stayed giving 24-hour care. After she died, I realised that I had been glad that I had been able to look after her in what must have been the worst time in her life. I realised that I had confidence in my ability to give her good care. Now, as I begin to think about my future, I feel that I would like to stay in Bristol and see whether I can re-train to work in Care. Your advertisement specifically said that you would provide training, so that is why I applied for work with the Council.'

Philippa with no more comment, asked 'I see from your application that you are forty-six years old. Would you mind giving us a brief outline of your employment history?'

'Well, I left school early, for personal reasons. I left home and moved to stay with my Aunt in Bristol. It was she who paid for me to take a Commercial Training course in the College of Commerce. I left with good qualifications in secretarial subjects including English Language, Typewriting and Pitman Shorthand. From there, over the years, I worked my way up. I started as a junior typist with an Agricultural Merchant in Avonmouth. I worked in two other companies each time applying for a more senior position. Eventually, when I was thirty I was offered a transfer to the NHS offices in Liverpool. When I left, I was Manager of Secretarial Services.'

'You showed real determination to get on in your chosen career. Do you see yourself having the same determination in Care work?' asked Jane.

'It's difficult for me to say that because I haven't worked professionally as a carer. However, if I felt that it was my vocation, then yes, I would look to progress.'

'Jennifer', said Janet softly, 'I see from the Health section of your application that you have experienced depression. Can you tell us how long this was for and the treatment you received. You don't have to share this with us if it is distressing. The reason that I ask is that other than the six months you were off work with depression, your sickness absence record is first class.'

94

Jennifer was quiet for a moment as though she was wondering whether she could share the past. She gently squared her shoulders and looking directly at all three interviewers she answered,

'I had a child when I was fifteen. That's why I moved away. My parents told me to leave and my Auntie took me in. I don't know what I would have done otherwise. The baby was adopted although I desperately wanted to keep her, but in those days, (thirty years ago), you didn't get much say in things. I experienced considerable bereavement feelings after she was taken away. The only thing I have of hers is the tiny identity bracelet they put on her wrist in hospital. My feelings caught up with me ten years later and I was absolutely overwhelmed with grief. I had counselling and have come to realise that I did what was best for my daughter and perhaps one day she will realise that and try to find me. However, I have been able to come to terms with the past and have been perfectly fine since.'

Philippa, looking up at Jennifer, said, 'Thank you for being so open with us Jennifer - are you able to answer one or two further questions? I am aware that we have rather put you on the spot as it were'.

'Please do, I'm fine, please carry on'.

'Let me give you a scenario. For some time, you have been visiting Mr Jones daily as his Support Worker. One morning you find him with a temperature and refusing to eat breakfast. You persuade him to have a drink and suggest that he has a visit from the doctor. He refuses point blank. What would you do?'

'I experienced this difficulty with my Auntie. There were times when she wouldn't accept my suggestion. I suppose in the end you have to accept that Mr Jones is an adult who is quite capable of making decisions for himself. I would explain my concerns but if he refused, I would have to accept that.'

'A good answer Jennifer', said Jane. 'We have no right whatsoever to inflict our will on another adult. What we would suggest you do in this situation is to explain fully the implications of his decision. For instance a temperature could be an indication of an infection which could become worse without treatment. You could also ring the office and ask that your programme of work is changed so that you can return at lunchtime to check on him.'

Janet looked up and asked Jennifer if there was anything she would like to ask of the panel. This she did. She needed to know more about the training on offer and the length of induction.

Janet brought the interview to a close in the usual way. As Jennifer made to leave the room, Jane was moved to say that she hoped Jennifer would one day meet her daughter.

Jennifer thanked her and said 'I don't hold out much hope really, as I only know two things about her. One is that today is her 30th birthday and the other is the name on the hospital bracelet, which was Philippa'.

Abanuea, Disappearing Island

Alan Beckett

Beach that is long lasting but now, shallow.
In the settled minds of simple fishermen,
Signs of silent changes in the skies below,
The rising fumes, plumes with no end.
Our ruthless, astounding exploitation.

Rolling waves, azure skies, warm, air borne
Aqueous vapour drives the World's weather engine.
Night and day the ocean swells but none mourn
The lost soldiers as sands turn and quicken,
The dead rising. Untimely resurrection.

White bony fingers plead to Helios
As the seas spread soil over their deep eyes,
The island is drowned in height and across.
Graveyards give up their rested, to die
Again in watery sublimation.

The climate of change has changed our climate.
Waves devour these little shores, savouring
Much more beyond this Pacific rim state.
The uprising bones of those who died fighting
Will return, floating by our front doors.

Is There A Place For Jimmy Badger

Barbara Calvert

The notion of friends and family had long ago moved into the back seat of Jimmy Badger's life. Once he'd had something approximating a family; maybe he still did. His mum would be getting on a bit; in her eighties at least, and his nan would most certainly have passed on by now. Truth to tell, from the age of 12, he'd always carried with him a niggling doubt as to whether she really was his nan. As a boy, family life had been, to say the least, transitory; marked out by one cheap flat or bed and breakfast after another, punctuated occasionally by being dropped off, like a bag of dirty laundry, on nan's doorstep. These visits usually ended with his mum's re-appearance, his newest 'uncle' in tow. The laundry bag was collected from nan and they were off again – 'til the next time.

One of the prison rituals he'd become used to, in his many and frequent stopovers in such places, was the well-intentioned visitor, whose mission it was to help Jimmy re-configure his life by sifting through the dregs of his childhood. Jimmy had been able to conjure up for his eager listeners a vivid, dream-like image of what life had felt like then. He described himself, holding his mum's hand – though in all honesty even this commonplace act of care and affection was more a tribute to Jimmy's imagination than any kind of reality. In his mind's eye they stood, hand in hand, watching a merry-go-round; its gaudy, galloping horses flashing past, round and round; then, as it slowed down, someone leapt off to join Jimmy and his mum. The horses carried on whirling around and before long that person, that 'uncle', leapt back on again, waved good bye, and was off on his unencumbered way. There was never space for Jimmy and his mum on the merry-go-round.

The prison visitors always liked that story and Jimmy had become a confident and colourful storyteller. Maybe if his frequent, but short, stays in prison had been a bit longer, this talent might have been nurtured and, who knows, could have been his salvation. But now it was too late.

Family, in his early days, had seemed small, insubstantial and fleeting, soon to evaporate entirely. At fifteen he'd left his mum by the merry-go-round for good and was not up to seeing himself as a bundle of unwashed clothes on nan's doorstep ever again.

As for friends, well, that was a roundabout too, but rarely merry. Never in one place for very long, he'd never acknowledged a gap in his life that needed filling by any particular human being. And none of those he met, drifters like himself, seemed to have spaces that were calling out for Jimmy to fill.

All the more amazing then, that just now Jimmy should be surrounded by thirty or more people whose sole reason for being there was to pay him due homage and respect. Father Murphy, prison chaplain, had brought together this gathering of obliging mourners, all of whom had found space in their lives for Jimmy Badger, now nailed down in his pale wooden coffin; pride of place at the gathering. Father Murphy's compassionate congregation, willing to turn out, when requested, for a man they'd never known; a man without a single friend or relative to bid him farewell.

Unable to bring to mind a picture of Jimmy, they nevertheless, wholeheartedly joined together to launch his careworn soul on to a better place. His last day on earth, by far his best ever, with the prayers of thirty total strangers rising up in unison to request a place for Jimmy Badger on heaven's perpetually spinning merry-go-round.

Prospect Lake

Ann Merrin

In the late evening the water had stilled. The canoe had nestled lightly between the large, smooth rocks at the edge of the lake. The last of the sun's light spread its pink glow across the sky and the still water. Peace had come again to Prospect Lake. And this was how it always was.

There were none now who could say when it had started. There were only stories that had been passed down from generation to generation. Myths. Legends. Horror stories.

Today Sean had kissed his wife goodbye as he always did, dry lips landing somewhere on her face. He picked up his briefcase and his overnight bag.

'See you on Thursday. Probably late. Don't bother with dinner.'

'Ok love. Have a good trip. Don't forget your vitamins. See you Thursday.'

Marilyn turned back to the kitchen sink, a contented smile on her face.

By the time Sean got to work his lips were balmed and he smelled of Ralph Lauren. He wafted past his secretary and asked her to follow him.

'Now then Maureen. Are we all set for today?'

'Yes Mr Green. You'll find the itinerary on your desk. Double room and dinner table all booked. Are you leaving straight away?'

'I think so. Any urgent messages? Anything in the post I should look at?'

'Nothing I can't deal with or that won't wait a couple of days.'

'Good girl. I'll be straight off then. See you Friday morning.'

Sean bounced along to the third floor where Olivia Fountain was waiting for him. She gave last minute instructions to her secretary and picked up her bags. She looked gorgeous. It was just as well they were carrying their bags or they might have been all over each other.

They made a good looking couple. Sean early forties, dark hair, immaculately groomed. Olivia mid-thirties, tall, willowy blonde. And they were clever. They had coordinated their diaries so carefully. The conference at Prospect Lake provided a chance to up their career CVs *and* to consummate what up to now had just been a raging lust.

She wasn't his first of course. It was an occupational hazard for Sean. He was constantly meeting beautiful women and he was pretty irresistible. Oh Marilyn was his first love, these others meant nothing to him. They came and went but Marilyn was always waiting at home for him. He knew that. He was sure of that.

When they arrived at the conference centre they were pleased to find that their rooms were conveniently adjacent. Each room contained a double bed (no doubt they'd both be well used), a bottle of wine, basket of fruit, and an envelope containing a voucher inviting them to a dinner for two at the lakeside. Maureen was only young, but she'd thought of everything.

Things were looking good. But the fun would have to wait, there was an opening talk to attend.

By five-thirty the Welcome Meeting was over and drinks were being served at the bar. Sean and Olivia smiled and small-talked for what they felt was an acceptable half hour, then, exchanging nods, they left.

The consummation beat all expectations. They were hot. They were insatiable. And by eight o'clock they were ready for their lakeside dinner.

The sun was low in the sky as they walked down toward the lake. They could see a table laid with silver cutlery, cut glass, a candle burning steadily in the still evening air. They were greeted by Julian, their waiter for the evening. The setting was perfect. As was the food, the champagne and the wines.

Around nine-thirty Julian summoned waiters to clear table and dishes away. The couple were left with a bottle of wine and an invitation to use the canoe at the water's edge. Sean was ecstatic!

'I haven't been canoeing since I was thirteen! Oh what a perfect evening for it! Olivia, my love, come sail with me.'

He grabbed her hands and she willingly followed him down to the water. She climbed in and sat against the cushions at the far end. She looked divine. Sean climbed in and used an paddle to push away from the shore. He paddled vigorously to begin with until they were in the middle of the lake, then he rested. They floated gently.

In contrast to the still water, their passions had begun to rise again. Sean moved from his seat and sat beside Olivia. They were soon naked and enjoying each other's bodies. In a climatic embrace they felt as though the world were spinning around them.

It was. The canoe had slowly started to twirl. And spin. Faster, then faster. Before the lovers realised it the canoe was spinning and lifting at one end. It lifted and lifted, until it stood on end. It was quite a sight to see – if anyone had been able to see it – as it pirouetted and tipped its contents into the lake. It slowed, and settled, and silently drifted off toward the shore.

The following morning Sean and Olivia were missed at breakfast. Phone calls were made to their rooms. Visits were made to their rooms. Their companies were contacted to see if an emergency had recalled them. Marilyn received a phone call. No, she thought her husband was still at the conference centre. And no, she didn't know a Miss Olivia Fountain. Oh dear.

The police had to be called in, but after three days there was no trace of either Olivia or Sean. No one had seen them after the Welcome Meeting. Marilyn was informed.

Maureen called in to see Marilyn. She'd brought some of Sean's 'effects' from his office.

'It must be such a shock to you Mrs Green. I can't believe it myself.'

'Well I do know that area Maureen. I was brought up around Prospect Lake, I know some strange things have happened around there. So, although it is a shock, well, I can't say I can't believe what's happened. Lots of people have gone missing around there you know.'

'I didn't know that. Do you know what might have happened to him then? It was strange, that Miss Fountain going missing too wasn't it?'

'Not really Maureen. Mr Green was known to spend time with other women you know.'

'No!' Maureen gasped.

'Yes Maureen. It was a shame about Miss Fountain, but then 'you can't make an omelette without breaking eggs'.'

Garden Of Memories

Patricia Welford

My memory garden begins with a flower called Sorrow
its perfume so lovely it compels and mesmerises
the star shaped head of petals seem as soft as full velvet
but are frosted crystals of pure brilliant ice-cold white.

Enticed I always touch the petal edges razor sharp
they cut causing pain so profound it makes my heart bleed
and to cry out, almost beyond endurance but I do endure
as the exquisite flower buds continue to grow potently
I am entrapped bewitched within their appalling beauty.

Lurking behind Sorrow there is a dire vine named Despair
with dense black leaves it grows strongly in the darkest corner
threatening tendrils spiralling menace await their chance
to encompass and drag my spirit to dread depression.

I have at times ventured trembling and anxious to its edge
hacking desperately attempting to destroy its growth
but the prolific morass defies my puny attempts
majestic in corner shade it grows on culled but mocking
its greedy demand for ground means we rage constant war.

Then wind wafted an exquisite aroma pervades my senses
attracted I take the path onwards to the flowering of Hope
delicate blue bells with gold stamen so appealing, I choose
to sit amongst the flowers cushioned upon its feathery tufts.

A distant kaleidoscopic display demands my attention
tall trumpets of Joy in triumphant oranges herald the sky
overflowing Passion bold bonnets of scarlet and crimson
Happiness great yellow heads each a child painted sun
My amazed eyes relish the razzle dazzle clash of colour.

Whilst here and nearby I can trace Loves' insistent ramblings
crowding the ground intermingling to flirt humouring stones
indestructible silken flutes stunning multi shaded purples
always busy smothering out Hate Anger Jealousy and Spite.

Cheered I follow the winding path to blooms of Contentment
whose rain drops of petals mass overlapping in abundance
delicious ruby with centres darkening to maroon and oblivion
I sink my nose deep inside an exquisite goblet dark as wine
inhaling the heavenly perfume is fulfilling but I cannot linger.

I step on with trust confident in the garden everlasting
within tumultuous emotions gentle compassion meanders
the hard stony path steadfast beneath my feet sustains me
with reflections on life's journey gathered in I am replete.

Refugees

Jenny Tunstall

That October, the smell of potatoes, dusty and sour in huge paper sacks, seemed the perfect antidote to my father's violent temper. Nothing as reliable as a good spud, my mother said with a shy smile, nothing as solid and dependable. I saw her stroke their misshapen curves, their rotten ends and spade gashes one afternoon, alone in the larder, while I finished drying up the lunch-things through in the strange, quarry-tiled kitchen. It was already a chilly place to be, but my mother's optimism was infectious and her new, bright smile nearly silenced my misgivings.

On September 29th 1982, my father threw a bread-knife at my mother, his stubbled cheeks stretched tight across his screaming face. I closed my eyes, heard her shriek and pictured red blood blossoming from her white face. Later I saw the door jamb, knife still embedded, and tried to block out his sobbing and begging as my mother packed her suitcase. A knife of fear pierced me when I realised that she was leaving us, but she caught my eye through my barely-open bedroom door and whispered *pack some clothes, not too many.*

Now we were seventy miles away, our cityscape replaced by blunt hills, our curse-strewn home replaced by a silent museum where chintz lived on, potatoes were still grown in small-holding rows and my grandparents prayed aloud before they ate any meal. They were virtual strangers to me, visited on rare occasions, never too bothered about liking me, the unwitting target of many of my father's cruder jokes.

My mother and I shared a room, two narrow beds, one locker, one chest of drawers with crocheted doily and free-standing mirror, one small wardrobe with temperamental key-mechanism and a sloping roof out of which a tiny window jutted, overlooking the herb garden, shed, hedge, lane and fields. My mother snored at night and muttered as she dreamed. I watched the circling of stars around the pole star through the gap at the bottom of the curtain, watched clouds swell and race across a growing moon, watched rain spatter on wrinkled glass and pushed hard against the approach of a new school day. I was the foreigner now, of no real address, a refugee, an interloper in a class where adolescent friendships were already sealed.

The kitchen was the most bizarre room in the house. Sometimes, looking round, I was surprised to see electric sockets at all. The gas stove had no pilot light or electric sparker, but was lit with a taper that Gran stuck through the part-open door of the coal-burner at the other end of the room. A slow walk, tiny flame cupped in her left hand, took her fifteen steps around the oval table to the stove, then hiss and *pleuph*! *Matches*, I wanted to say. *Have you not heard?* She minced Sunday's left over roast meat in a hand-cranked mill, clamped to the table edge, beef one week, lamb the next, never pork because grandfather didn't like it. Cottage pie one week, shepherd's pie the next, rich in gravy, rounded with dusty white potato, lifted from one of the sacks, peeled in a bowl of filthy water, boiled to extinction and mashed briefly with a fork. I peeled them, hands aching in the cold water, feeling the scales of peelings accumulate in the soft folds between my fingers and the mud settle under my nails. I tried peeling them dry. We never made mistakes more than once in Gran's kitchen.

I couldn't understand it. If someone had thrown a bread-knife at me, my mother would have been outraged on my behalf, fired with sympathy and support. Her parents had never been demonstrative, she said.

I peeled potatoes on Mondays, Wednesdays and Fridays and my mother did the other days. I thought of my father while I peeled. How he would laugh, teasing me, despising my mother. He had thrown an ash-tray at me once and then laughed because I batted it away with a plimsoll I happened to have in my hand and he shouted *rounder!* My heart pumped as though I had run round every base, but it swelled too, at his praise. There was only one phone at Gran's house, an old green one with a round dial, on a table in the hall, all doors opening on to it, all ears within reach. I didn't phone him.

The larder was filled as I had seen display cases in museums filled, orderly, every space used sensibly, every item labelled. Top shelf jams and chutneys not yet in use; blackberry, raspberry, gooseberry; apple jelly, quince jelly, apple chutney, tomato chutney, each jar dated, each label facing forward. Next shelf tins, sardines, soup, beans, spam, golden syrup as yet unopened, all tins ranged to perfection, savoury and sweet segregated, small to large, labels staring straight ahead. At floor-level were the sacks of produce; carrots, parsnips, potatoes, onions hung from hooks, apples stacked in pallets, arranged so that no two apples touched, each pallet labelled with variety, tree, date of picking. Apple sharpness merged with bready sweetness, but always the green hint of rot from the potato sacks dominated.

Gran and Grandfather spoke to each other in calm, polite tones. They thanked each other, greeted each other, proffered assistance in language that needed no adaptation at the Methodist Chapel next door, where they spent every spare moment. They were cool with each other in correct and measured love. My mother praised them for it in the privacy of our bedroom blackout. I wondered whether the elation of her escape blinded her to their disapproval or whether their unwillingness to eff and blind at her, throw heavy objects at her or, indeed, to drink themselves senseless, was such balm and relief that their unwelcoming silences were taken as deliberate attempts at solace. Her bruises faded, her shoulders straightened and her face regained a little colour. She stopped flinching at sudden movements caught in the periphery of her vision.

As I wrestled with simultaneous equations and the Franco-Prussian war, she dug her way across Grandfather's two acres until her back ached. I rubbed it for her at night while she checked my homework. I dug with her on Saturdays. It was endless and not even rain put a stop to it. Grandfather kept digging and so did we, fingers aching with cold. Worse came with the washing of the winter curtains which had to be ironed to perfection (no steam iron), ready for hanging and then the washing of the summer curtains that had to be ironed ready for winter storage. *No*, I said, *not ironed to be folded and squashed on to a closet shelf.* Gran's lips pressed together as though they intended to bond permanently and I ironed.

My mother had worked in a Building Society on our town's High Street, had lunched each day with friends, had her hair dyed every four weeks, had bought clothes with money left over each month, had danced at office Christmas Do's and phoned friends for chats most evenings. Then, for the last year at home, I could see her fading, her colours paling, her hair greying, her clothes somehow muting, but I thought it was her age and then I knew it was my father. As the colour began to return to her face at Gran's I waited silently for her hair to darken and her old smile to grow again.

I heard muttered conversations in the dining room while I was in the larder; heard beseeching tones unanswered in the kitchen while I was in the cold bathroom overheard; heard muffled sobs in our twin-bedded darkness on several nights.

'But why?' I demanded, late one night.

I heard her sigh in the darkness.

'Because I have broken my wedding vows.'

'What?'

'"For better or for worse". They think I have broken up our home, your home.'

'But he threw a knife at you. Didn't he vow to love and cherish you? That one's pretty broken now.'

'He must answer to God for his failure and I must answer to God for mine. That's how they see it.'

I smouldered silently. Their own daughter. I hated them for not loving her and I despised her for not hating them.

The Christmas season saw us dragged inexorably into the midst of the Methodists, some jovial and so kind they made my throat ache, some puzzled and distant, some stern, of Gran and Grandfather's unpleased demeanours. We sang carols, bewildered by the outbreak of sung harmonies around us; lit candles stuffed into oranges and watched children try to ignite each other with them; held sway over a bric-a-brac stall at the Christmas fair, always together, always bracketed, treated as each other's equal, two displaced and uncomfortable adolescents. I was surprised she took it all and then came Christmas itself.

The solitary old people of several villages were rounded up and brought to the Chapel hall for Christmas Day lunch, prepared and cooked in Gran's kitchen. We peeled potatoes and carrots and parsnips, trimmed and crossed sprouts, mixed bowls of stuffing and shelled chestnuts from dawn until dusk on Christmas Eve and barely snatched a *Happy Christmas* before being shepherded to Chapel the next morning. We sang, smiled, bowed our heads, all as expected, then donned our aprons and obediently served. My knuckles cracked and split into gashes, my legs ached from standing for so many hours on the quarry tiles and my head ached with the longing for home and a proper Christmas. My mother's smile was too bright all day and from the angle of her shoulders I could tell that her back was screaming at her as we lugged back to Gran's kitchen sink forty-seven soup bowls, forty-seven dinner plates, forty-seven Christmas pudding plates, nearly two hundred spoons, forks, knives and serving implements, forty-seven cups, forty-seven saucers, jugs, pans, lids, basins and roasting tins. The sweat ran down our temples and necks, into our cleavages and down our spines. Tea towels became sodden, the back-boiler failed to keep up with our need for hot water and whenever it was my turn to wash, I found my hands greased by the dish water and mobbed by the detritus that had escaped forty-seven pairs of dentures. We tried to sing, but our carols sounded too much like the Spirituals of other slaves.

Finally Grandfather appeared to help us carry the dishes back to the Chapel for storage until the next church supper. We lugged, stacked and straightened, one eye on Grandfather's face, waiting breathlessly for some sign of approval. Back on the quarry tiles we wiped surfaces and tidied in silence. I folded seven wet tea towels and stacked them on the draining board. My mother declared that we deserved some mince pies and a cup of tea and dragged herself into the larder to find them. I turned to find Gran watching me and I raised the corners of my mouth at her.

'Reverend Morgan was asking about you,' she said. I pictured him, tall in his long black gown, the white of his dog-collar almost hidden in the white of his beard. 'He pities you, child.'

Kindness was bad enough.

'He has no reason to pity her.' My mother's voice was muffled. Her head was down and her back turned.

'She is homeless, socially disadvantaged, let-down.'

The last of my mother's optimism hissed out of her with a sigh that shook and curled into a sob deep in her chest. She turned slowly, tears hanging from her lower lids. I remembered the wedding photos then. A bride of eighteen, surrounded by young friends and a handsome rake of a new husband, his mother already lighting her next cigarette, his uncle not bothering to conceal his hip-flask; her parents, two sober dark marks far right.

There was a strange choking sound from her lips suddenly and I smelt the flat pungency of the potato sack a split second before her arm whipped over and the crash of smashing willow-patterned pottery made me flinch. My grandmother did not move. The second potato brought a cascade of copper jelly moulds, the third, close to my grandmother, knocked the lid from the butter-dish and I saw the pale cow roll from the top and hide beneath the dresser. The fourth thudded against the darkening window and the fifth found the empty milk bottles at the back of the draining board. To every angle from her larder stronghold, my mother fired potatoes, reserving only two areas, mine and her mother's. With every throw she grunted, a little higher each time, demanding reaction, each key change a sign of lessening control, each throw harder, more serious, more intent. My heart pounded and I trembled with the horror of witnessing this inexorable walk to the line of sanity and across it. With each pause I thought she might stop, with each new throw I watched her approaching ever closer the point of no return. Then, mind made up, she paused to take aim and hurled her final potato. It struck her mother on the breast. Finally there was a gasp, a hand clutched to the pain. A whiteness of silent, clamped-down rage. A closed door and an emptiness. A long moment of nothingness, ground won, battle done. And then my mother sobbing, quietly, hopelessly, face buried in her soaked apron, knees on the quarry tiles, head against the larder door-jamb. I inhaled the fresh stench of raw potato juice and watched her weep.

Wise Words

Patricia Lloyd

Alex turned the sign to 'Open' and unlocked the door. She stepped outside into the cold Spring air and looked along the road. There was no sign of life and the only sound breaking the quiet, was that of the occasional hum of a passing car. This was her favourite time of the day. The quiet of night, waiting expectantly, for the rhythm of day to begin.

Shortly, people on the early shifts at the nearby mill, would call in for paper and cigarettes. Very soon after would come those who are retired, taking an early morning constitutional to collect the daily paper and very often a bag of humbugs. Between eight and nine would see a mix of customer, children calling in for snacks or an assortment of sweets on the way to school, office workers picking up cigarettes and something for their lunch and finally mothers on the way home from taking children to school, looking for the ingredients for a meal. Better get on, she thought as she picked up the large parcel of newspapers left by the shop door.

As she undid the papers and began to sort them, Alex heard her grandmother moving about in the cottage behind the shop. She had come to live with Gran when she had been taken suddenly ill and was no longer able to run her village shop. At the time Alex had just taken her 'A' levels at school. Her planned gap year of travel to the Far East had been cancelled and she had travelled instead from her home in London to stay with Gran in the small village of Westonwood near the coast at Lyme Regis.

'Breakfast is ready love' Gran said, putting her head round the doorway. 'You go first – I'll have mine afterwards.' Gran and Alex never sat to eat breakfast or lunch together because one of them was usually serving in the shop. In the evenings they made up for it by enjoying a leisurely meal together – that was if Alex was not going out.

Sitting at the breakfast table, Alex had one thought on her mind – the coming reunion of her tutor group at school. It wasn't that she didn't want to see all her old friends. She really looked forward to that part. What really concerned her was the fact that they had all done so well and she had been content to stay on here with Gran and virtually take over the shop. She had made significant changes to the shop – modernised the fittings, improved the variety of stock and trebled the turnover. What was all that compared to Jodie, now a GP and Tim who was a solicitor? Here she was at twenty-five running her Gran's shop. She had originally intended to do an English degree and had received an offer from Bristol University.

Gran wanted her to go to the reunion – had even suggested a new outfit for the occasion. She could return home to stay with Mum and Dad and, as the reunion was being held in the school, would be able to walk to it if necessary.

Later, while driving back from the Cash and Carry, Alex realised that her main concern was meeting with Tom again. They had had 'a thing' going in the sixth form. They were close friends and spent a good deal of time together but had never actually become 'a couple'. Gran's sudden illness and her move to Lyme Regis had put a stop to that.

Initially, they had telephoned each other and written the odd letter. He had even visited once, but his move to Edinburgh University and her involvement with the shop meant that the relationship came to nothing. I wonder what he's doing now, she thought. He was going to be a psychiatrist. They had been such close friends. They were able to talk about anything. She missed that. There had been no-one in her life since with whom she had felt so comfortable.

As she unloaded the car and carried stock into the shop she decided that she was being a wimp. If she didn't go she would always regret it. What was the matter with her? Was it living out here in the wilds – had she lost the knack of conversation and mixing out of her comfort zone? She would go. After all if she didn't enjoy it she wouldn't have far to walk home!

It was a warm July evening when Alex walked the street leading to Fairview Comprehensive. She could see the gym building between the houses at the end of the road.

Cars passed her heading in the same direction but no one acknowledged her presence. The new shoes with their high heels were beginning to pinch and she felt very alone. She could see the arched doorway which led into the main hall. A few people were milling around outside greeting each other.

A tall man was stood to one side leaning against the wall. He had one leg bent behind him – his foot flat against the wall. She remembered that stance. She knew without a doubt it was Tom and he was waiting for her. He came towards her smiling, took her hand and said, 'I'm so glad to see you.' All she could say in reply was, 'Me too.'

Later, back in Westonwood over coffee, Alex told Gran all about it. She told her about walking into the hall with Tom at her side and the difference it had made to her. She became happy and confident and able to talk to everyone there. What she hadn't expected was the attendance of some of their old tutors.

She had been pleased to see Miss Jennings again – the person she believed gave her a love of books and English literature. Miss Jennings had told her that she kept up as best as she could with the lives of her ex pupils. She had heard a great deal about Alex from a friend who was in the Dorset Chamber of Commerce.

It had been noted how Alex had taken over her Grandmother's village store and turned it into 'Village Stores Ltd' a co-operative offering struggling village outlets a joint stock-purchasing scheme. The co-operative had been able to block purchase stock at fair prices. Was it really true that Alex had supported four stores that had been on the verge of closure? Alex had shyly told her that it was so. She had been congratulated by Miss Jennings for achieving so much in so little time.

'Rightly so' said Gran.

Alex then told her that she would always remember what Miss Jennings said at the end of their conversation, ' 'It's not the qualifications we have that make the difference to our lives, it's the decisions we make' and that quote Alex comes from a Harry Potter book written by a very successful woman.'

At that point Gran and Alex were interrupted in their conversation, by their very new shop assistant Tom, who, swinging around the door-jamb asked;

'I've a customer who wants something called Friar's Balsam. Anyone know what and where it is?'

Gran and Alex broke into laughter as Alex got up to find the remedy.

His Absence

Jenny Tunstall

He is gone: goodbye is over
And the echoes have stilled;
Silence fills the rooms where he should be.
Wandering through them restlessly,
I grasp remembered sounds;
A laugh, a song
His gently softened vowels.
He is gone and will, of course, return.
But in this void,
This eternal moment between
The sadness and the joy,
We must all wait;
His piano, unplayed,
His book, unread,
His pillow, undented,
His wife, unkissed.
He is gone; my love is gone;
And he is missed.

Follow Your Stars

Ann Merrin

ARIES: Adventurous day. Do you feel like having an adventure?
Well today, you're likely to have an adventure when you go on a short
journey. No need to go very far, just someplace you've wanted to go
before, yet never been. Today is also a good day to surprise a close
friend with news or a small gift.

Gordon read it through several times. Well, this was certainly
a strong message. He had a completely clear day, where should he go?
He'd never been on the channel ferry, which he could see from his
living room window, sailing in and out. That was hardly a 'short
journey' though. No, he'd probably stay closer to home.

What about one of those boat trips round Herring Island? Now
that sounded more like it. He finished his breakfast, washed the dishes
and set out across the Quay. It was already busy. In the tourist season
it was rarely anything else. He found several boats offering similar
trips but decided on the Island Queen, because he liked the name.

With an hour to spare before sailing he took a stroll along the
Quay and stopped for coffee at one of his regular haunts. Joyce, the
waitress, commented that he was in early today and he told her what
he was up to.

'I've always fancied that trip. Never done it. I suppose you
don't when you live in a place.'

'Why don't you come today?' said Gordon, feeling suddenly
bold on his adventurous day out.

'Well Cath won't be in for another half hour, I won't have
time.'

'No, it's ok, it doesn't leave until eleven. I could pop along
and get a ticket for you if you like.'

'Oh, go on then! I'm going to throw caution to the wind. Let's
go!' She was infected by his spirit of adventure.

Gordon finished his coffee and strode off to buy another ticket. What a day this was turning out to be!

The boat left promptly at eleven. It was a popular trip and Gordon and Joyce just managed to get a seat together. The day was perfect: sunshine, blue skies and a calm sea. There was a running commentary pointing out things that, as locals, they had never seen.

At twelve o'clock the boat docked at the island and everyone got off for lunch. The pair agreed that they were having a great day. They bought some sandwiches and walked along the cliff path. They had an hour to spend looking around the island.

They sat on a bench and enjoyed their lunch. Looking out over the sea as it glittered green and blue; listening to the waves splashing and the sea birds calling; breathing the clear, clean air. Gordon thought he had never been happier in his life. And Joyce? Joyce just glowed. It had been a perfect day.

They decided to walk on a little further and were surprised to see someone walking towards them. For some reason they had come to think that they were the only people on the island. Silly really. But here was someone walking purposefully towards them. As they came close Gordon recognised a man in rather unusual dress. A hippy probably. As they neared each other all three stopped.

The stranger looked intently at them both. And they looked back at him. No one spoke. The stranger wore baggy trousers and a long, loose jacket. Definitely a hippy. Then he smiled. His eyes sparkled and his face shone. Both Gordon and Joyce felt his warmth flow over them. For some reason they giggled and said what a lovely day it was.

He smiled again. And when he spoke his voice seemed to come from somewhere deep inside.

'I wonder what news you will have to impart after your adventurous day out?' he said, looking at them quizzically.

And, without waiting for an answer, he strode on. Gordon stood with his mouth agape.

'Well, for goodness sake! How did he know about that?'

'About what?' Joyce asked.

And so Gordon explained how his decision to come on this trip had come about.

120

'And then at the end of the horoscope it said something about bringing a close friend news or a gift. How on earth could *he* have known about that?' he said as he nodded towards the disappearing figure.

'Well I don't know. But guess what? I'm an Aries too.'

Gordon and Joyce agreed that they'd certainly followed their stars today. They talked about the things they'd seen and how they might well have been just sat indoors watching telly, missing all of the simple joys life had to offer.

Although the pair had known each other for years, they'd never really spent any time together. Their conversations had always involved the weather or the types of cakes on offer at the café. But today they began to find out a little about each other's lives. And the time just ran away with them.

When Gordon looked at his watch it was three-thirty! They ran back along the coast path to the dock where the boat *should* have been. Gone. Now what?

They made their way to the shop where they'd bought their sandwiches. The man behind the counter just smiled. It happened from time to time, he told them, they would just need to wait for the next boat. All the tour operators were prepared for taking back a couple of 'strays'. The next boat was due at four thirty, so they sat and had a cup of tea and laughed about 'missing the boat'

Seeing them giggling, the shopkeeper asked them if they'd met anyone on their walk.

'Yes, we did,' said Gordon. 'I wonder if you know him. He was quite tall and looked like a hippy.'

'Did he speak to you?'

'Yes. In actual fact he said something that surprised me greatly. He's a most unusual man.'

'Indeed he is, sir. He doesn't speak to many people. And not many people even see him. I can tell you – you've been blessed. The man is known on the island as The Astrologer. He's been here for many years. He comes and goes, but when he appears, it's always counted as a blessing. He just seems to spread an aura of peace and joy as he passes through.'

'So, what do you mean then? Is he a sort of ghost?!'

'Sort of. No one really knows for sure.'

'Well I'll be!' In all his life Gordon could never remember such a strange day. It was certainly a day he would never forget. And neither would Joyce. In fact Joyce had already decided on the 'news' she would be passing on.

When they were standing again on the Quay, Joyce shook Gordon's hand and thanked him profusely for a wonderful day out. Gordon was a little taken aback, he had imagined they might have tea together before parting. But he quietly thanked her for her company and walked slowly home. Perhaps he'd got too carried away with the excitement of the day.

The following morning his stars read: *ARIES: Be prepared for disappointment today. It won't be a lasting disappointment – as long as you follow your heart. Go out Aries and be bold!*

Gordon smiled. After the results of yesterday's horoscope, he felt his 'boldness' increasing. He finished his breakfast and took a casual stroll towards the Quay Café. He thought he might just catch up with Joyce, see how she was feeling today.

He was taken aback to find the café closed and near devastated to see the sign board had been taken down. They could never have sold up and moved out overnight! He walked on by, trying to imagine what might have happened. Perhaps Joyce had gone back to the island in search of The Astrologer. Perhaps she'd thought he'd been too forward yesterday. (Although he was sure he hadn't.) Perhaps it was something that had been planned for ages and she just hadn't mentioned it yesterday. What a disappointment.

For the next three days he didn't bother with the horoscopes, but he did walk past the Quay Café. It was Saturday when he next saw Joyce. There she was standing proudly outside on the pavement.

'I've been waiting for you,' she said to Gordon. 'What do you think?'

Gordon looked up to where she was pointing. There was a brand new sign. The café was now called 'Smiles'. And Joyce had the biggest smile as she took his arm and led him inside. The café had transformed. The seating was now made up of comfortable sofa's and low tables, and the walls were the colour of the sea just outside the window.

'This is all thanks to you Gordon.'

'Me? Well I've not done anything.'

''Not done anything! If you hadn't invited me out the other day, I might never have decided to go ahead with all this. Cath had been thinking of retiring for some time now and she'd offered the café to me at a *very* reasonable price. Well, I had the money but I wasn't sure whether I wanted the responsibility. And then that day, that strange day, it all fell into place. This is where I've been happiest. And this is where I met you. You see Gordon, that day helped me to recognise what was important in life. All I had to do was reach out and take it. I couldn't wait to get back to see Cath.'

'Oh Joyce, this is beautiful. And there was me thinking perhaps I'd offended you in some way. I'm so relieved and so happy for you.'

Joyce had closed the café door behind them. She led Gordon to one of the comfy seats and brought over a tray of coffee and Danish pastries.

Who knows how long they sat there that day but I can tell you this: it certainly wasn't the last time. They still check their horoscope and have never been afraid to follow their stars.

Human Resource

Alan Beckett

It felt strange attending a job interview on the Sabbath but needs must, thought Sally as she pushed open the door.

'Good afternoon, Miss Harbord. My name is Veronica Vansittart from HR. I will be conducting your first interview,' she said, slowly looking Sally up and down. 'Please be seated.'

'Hello,' said Sally, straightening her skirt and taking off her sunglasses.

'I see that you're applying for the recruitment manager position,' said the interviewer studying Sally's application.

'Hopefully,' Sally said. That was a bit limp she thought to herself. Need to be more assertive. She cleared her throat. 'Yes, definitely. That's the position I'm after.'

'Good,' replied the interviewer, shooting a quick smile at the attractive, young applicant. 'My job is to check your application and ask you some questions pertinent to the position. After a blood test you will then go on to see our senior haematology consultant who will speak with you. If he decides that you have a suitable attitude he will then require you to take a short practical test.'

'Oh! OK. That's fine,' replied Sally, trying hard to hide her surprise. Suitable *attitude* she said to herself. Surely she means *aptitude*?

Veronica shifted some papers around. 'I have copies of your annual reports and your nursing qualifications here and I must say they are very impressive. I see here that you have been involved in the stem cell harvesting program. Good.'

'Yes,' Sally perked up. 'I'm very interested in haematology and I would like to specialise.' Sally shifted forward in her seat feeling a little more confident. 'It would be a good experience starting at the source so to speak,' she tried to stifle a nervous giggle.

The interviewer looked up at Sally her eyes fixed and cold. 'Hum. Quite,' she replied.

Sally studied Veronica Vansittart. She was around ten years older than her but quite stunning in a gothic sort of way with raven black hair and sparkling green eyes. Her face seemed to glow like white marble in the dappled light of the small recruitment hall.

Sally could see a couple of other candidates waiting. A door at the end of the hall had an 'Interview in Progress' notice on it. The young girl that she had briefly spoken to in the corridor earlier on had just finished having her blood test after talking with Veronica and was being escorted through to see the consultant.

'So, Miss Harbord,' Veronica said, making direct eye contact with Sally. 'Everything seems to be in order. Now if you don't mind, just a few general questions.'

'OK, fine,' Sally replied, smiling at Veronica. So far so good she thought to herself.

'Should you be successful, where do see yourself in five years time?'

Sally thought for a moment and realised that this was one of *those* questions. The National Blood Service is always suffering from a high turnover and will be looking for people with commitment so she decided to give a political rather than an honest answer.

'Providing there are good prospects for promotion and self sustainment I believe I would be prepared to remain in this post.'

'Fine,' Veronica grunted, ticking a box. 'You do realise that there will be a considerable amount of travelling when we are on a national donor tour. You may also be required to travel to Eastern Europe.'

'Er… that's… OK,' Sally replied, with some hesitation. *Europe,* she thought, that's odd. 'I love travelling,' she quickly added.

'I assume that you are fully trained in phlebotomy and familiar with catheter insertion and transfusion methods?'

'Yes. I've had experience in that area for at least two years,' Sally replied.

'Have you ever taken venous or arterial drains from places other than the arms?' asked the interviewer, but she could see that Sally was puzzled. 'Let's say, the jugular vein or the carotid artery?'

'No! That's quite unusual isn't it?'

'Indeed.' Veronica replied. She did not tick the box.

Sally thought that this may have been another trick question but had decided to give the expected answer. She had to be sure. She really needed this job.

'Do you suffer from any blood related diseases?' the interviewer added.

'No,' Sally answered. The questions seem to be coming from all directions, she thought. Perhaps it was their interviewing technique, just to throw you off guard.

'Do you follow any religious faith that you feel may compromise you in the execution of the work?' Veronica continued.

'No,' Sally responded.

'Good.' She ticked a box. 'How do you feel about night work?'

'Been doing it for years,' Sally replied. This is a breeze, she thought.

Veronica Vansittart ticked off another box.

'Have you any close friends or relatives whom you see on a regular basis and who depend on you in any way?'

'Excuse me but that is an odd thing to ask,' said Sally.

Veronica looked up at the girl and stared at her for a moment. She smiled and started to read out the next question.

'No!' Sally interrupted. 'I already work anti-social hours and consequently there is no one who would miss me, more is the pity.'

'I see,' replied Veronica going back to tick the box.

Sally sat there for another ten minutes answering odd questions that seem to bear little relevance to the post. Finally the interviewer stood up and took her over to an elderly nurse who quickly took a blood sample from Sally. When this was concluded Veronica beckoned to her and started walking back towards the end of the hall.

'Come this way please. I would like you to meet someone.'

As Sally followed, it suddenly occurred to her that the girl, who went in before her a few minutes ago, had not come out yet. She assumed that there must be another exit.

Veronica ushered Sally through the door and into a small ante-room. The first thing she noticed were the drawn curtains blocking out the daylight. The second thing she noticed was that the girl who went in earlier was stretched out on a recovery bed in the corner of the room unconscious. Sally threw a quick glance in her direction before sitting down.

'Hello, Miss Harbord,' said the Doctor, shaking her hand. His grip was cold and limp and due to the dimness of the room she could not clearly see him behind his desk. Sally again glanced towards the girl on the bed.

'My name is Dr Bacau, Vladimir Bacau. Tut! Much bad manners, I assume I may call you Sally, yes? From where I come from in Romania we are much more direct in conversation.' The doctor noticed Sally glancing over towards the girl. 'Please do not be alarmed by that poor girl. The silly thing just passed out. Stress of the interview I think. She'll be fine soon, most unsuitable for the job, but fine.

'Oh!' Sally said, feeling tongue tied and a little surprised at the doctor's blasé attitude.

'Now you are err... how you say... another fishy kettle. Your CV is most excellent and a high motivation potential, exactly what we are looking for...' The consultant stopped in mid sentence as Veronica leaned over and whispered into his ear.

'Ah! I see,' he said as she returned to her position behind Sally. 'Hum. My dear, although your interview was on the whole very successful you seem not to be very clear regarding one of the questions on the err... how you say, blood-letting techniques.

'Yes, I know. I was uncertain,' Sally replied, a little nervous, 'but to be truthful I have in fact carried out this technique on a few occasions but only when it has been necessary and there were no other safer options.'

'I see,' grunted Dr Bacau. He stood up and walked around the desk coming into full view of Sally's gaze. He was tall, clean shaven and with a mauve complexion. There also seemed to be something wrong with his mouth. Perhaps an old encounter with a violent patient, perhaps a war wound, Sally mused.

'This is very interesting, Sally.' Dr Bacau picked up a poster displaying the human circulatory system. 'Just to clear up any misunderstandings would you show me on this diagram where you would make an incision, let's say around the patient's neck region.'

The Doctor looked up at Veronica who was pointing her head in the direction of the girl still lying unconscious on the bed.

'Yes. Still better, maybe you could just show us on this unfortunate whilst she is still in nodding land. She will not mind.

Disturbed by the unethical approach of the interviewers, Sally was not prepared to show her hand this early but she was so hungry for this position she reluctantly walked over to the prone form on the bed. She immediately traced her finger lightly along the girl's skin indicating where she would make an incision.

'Correct Miss Harbord but please, demonstrate to us *exactly* how you would affect an entry,' Veronica urged, smiling at Dr Bacau who was slowly moving up behind Sally.

Confident that she had now secured the job Sally glanced back at the pair and turned towards the girl's throbbing jugular.

'What the hell,' Sally whispered to herself and expertly sunk her canines into the girl's neck sucking at and then stemming the sudden gush of blood. She then pinched off the twin flows with a complex gripping arrangement of her fingers. 'Like this?' Sally said coyly, as warm, fresh blood trickled down her chin.

'Most excellent,' the Doctor hissed. 'You've got the job. Can you start tonight?'

Discovery

Ann Merrin

Supposing you discovered -
a hoard of buried treasure?
Do you think that it would change your life?
Give you pleasure without measure?

Supposing you discovered -
a lying and cheating spouse?
Would you commit a crime of passion?
Or be a mouse to that foul louse?

Supposing you discovered –
you had a long lost brother?
Would you welcome him with open arms?
Or not want to share your mother?

Supposing you discovered –
Truth and the Meaning of Life?
Do you think it would end the struggle?
Bring you Paradise, free from strife?

No, my friends listen closely:
Never give up on the quest.
Life is all about discovery
Then deciding what you like best!

Heddwch

Patricia Lloyd

The picture is about eighteen inches wide and nine inches deep. It's a landscape – a painting of my childhood home. I lived on a small farm in the welsh mountains – that is, until my mother died.

The picture shows our farmhouse, the barn alongside it and the lake behind. These are shown in the distance as though the artist is painting while standing on top of Sugar Loaf (our mountain). Woodland lies below the place where the artist is painting and fields of corn and beet take the eye to my home.

'Heddwch' was the name of this place when I lived there. Its meaning in English is 'Peace'. Our home was a simple croft. Stone built, flag flooring and all the inconveniences the holidaymakers knew nothing about.

I think it must have been my grandmother who named the croft because it certainly wasn't a place of peace during my childhood.

Mother and Father were in their late thirties when they married. I believe it was because my father needed help to care for his elderly parents and Mother didn't want to be 'left on the shelf'. I don't believe anything like love was involved.

There was never anything like raised voices or bad language in our home but the atmosphere was citric. I was born soon after their marriage and as neither had any experience of children before; the term 'raised myself' comes to mind when I think of my childhood. Very little was said to me unless it was an instruction to do something. I received kindness from my grandfather when I was small, but he died just before my eighth birthday. My Nana died before him.

My father received a small inheritance from his parents and used this to renovate one of the outbuildings into holiday accommodation.

This holiday 'cottage' had all the modern conveniences expected by holidaymakers and with its views of the lake and the mountain was rarely empty in the tourist season.

When I finished school it became my task to clean the cottage and ensure our guests had everything they needed. My parents weren't comfortable with strangers and therefore left these tasks to me.

No-one visiting the farm would have known or even sensed the hatred that bred in our home. Both my parents bitterly regretted being landed with the other for the rest of their lives. They never missed a chance to ridicule or belittle one another. I grew up in the middle of it all. Both of them used me to assuage their anger. With my mother it was the physical stuff. She would slap and kick me for not working hard or quick enough.

From my father I received verbal abuse which was supposed to reduce my self worth. It had the reverse effect. The hatred I had for him gave me strength. When I was young I wanted to run away but I had no-one and nowhere to run to.

When I was twelve I decided that I would bide my time. I would collect what money I could towards my future and eventually free myself. I worked hard at school but exams and further education was not allowed as I was needed to work at home. I saved every penny I earned from various odd jobs around the village. I studied and read night after night as I set about my planning my freedom.

Now as I look at the picture before throwing it into the skip I'm glad that I can discard my home so easily. I have an inheritance now. I've sold the farm – there is money in my bank account. I knew as a child that I had been left the farm, because Nana told me that Grandfather bypassed Father in his will and left everything to me with the proviso that Mother and Father could live on the farm for life.

I have my own boat now. Watching my father row out to the middle of the lake used to fill me with envy. I would love to have been out there all alone, at peace. When I could, I learned to sail and bought my first dinghy. It's ironic I suppose that Father died out there in the middle of the lake.

He drowned you know. It's thought that his boat sprang a leak and he couldn't get back to shore. It's a shame, isn't it, that Father never learned to swim?

Mother died the following year. She was in her early fifties. I introduced her to the benefits of herbal remedies. There are many wild plants around the farm and she took to producing her own concoctions. I bought her special herbs which did not grow locally. The doctor thought that she had taken too much of one particular plant which could, if taken in large quantities, affect the liver.

The estate agent said that it was a tragedy that they died so close together and at such a young age. I suppose it depends on how you define tragedy doesn't it?

The Green Umbrella

Maureen Nicholls

Lady Grainger was about to leave the house when, almost as an after thought, she stopped and asked the footman to run and fetch her daughter from the nursery. While she waited, she eased her fingers into a pair of long green kid gloves, only looking up as the child approached.

'Ah, Georgie, come, give me a kiss goodbye.' She proffered her cheek. 'Now I want you to be a good girl for Mamma.' She pinched her little daughter's chin and turned to the waiting footman.

'Is it raining, Higgs?' She asked.

'Not at the moment my Lady, but it's not looking good. Shall I fetch the carriage?'

'No need. I'm not going far, I'll take an umbrella.'

Georgina ran to the hall stand. 'Take your green one Mamma, it matches your gloves.' She held it out to her mother.

'So it does, how clever of you, Georgie darling.'

The elegant umbrella had a tall tapering handle of rich creamy ivory, supporting an intricate frame of spokes, all encased in the finest green silk. Georgina loved to play with it, ignoring Nanny who said it was bad luck to put up an umbrella indoors; she paraded round and round beneath it, the light shining through the green silk giving a strange, under-sea effect.

Lady Grainger blew her daughter a kiss and left the house. She was never to return.

In the servants' quarters, talk was all about a strange gentleman who called at odd hours when his Lordship was away and complaints from her ladyship's maid who had been made to wait on park benches, while her mistress rode off in a strange carriage for hours on end.

To Georgina, her Mamma's prolonged absence was not a matter of great concern, although she missed having the green umbrella to play with and she disliked the way servants ceased their

135

conversations abruptly whenever she appeared. However, she still had Nanny, who was the most important person in her small world.

Nanny, despite the gossip, was sure something terrible had happened to her Ladyship. It was she who had begged his Lordship to call out the Police force and after twenty-four hours, with no word from his wife, Lord Grainger was forced to agree. The investigating officer was a Detective from the newly formed Metropolitan Police and with quiet persistence and gentle questioning, soon got to the bottom of the servants' gossip, most of which he disregarded as conjecture about a mistress who was obviously disliked. However, he did think it odd that the missing Lady had taken what, for her, was the unusual step of sending for Georgina before leaving the house that day. Even the loyal Nanny asserted she was not known to be a particularly affectionate mother.

Lady Grainger's sister had been less than helpful in assisting with his enquiries. Her abhorrence of any intrusion into her family by someone she regarded as no better than a servant, was made appallingly plain. Any suggestion that her sister might be in danger, she considered laughable.

'It is obvious to me,' she said, 'that she must have taken an extended holiday abroad and forgotten to tell her stuffy husband - such a fuss about nothing!'

She refused to be questioned further by the Detective and, when asked by Lord Grainger himself if she knew anything about her sister's whereabouts, denied all knowledge and declared she had nothing more to say on the subject.

Privately, the Detective was sure that Lady Daymar knew exactly where her sister was and was obviously untroubled by any fear of her having met with harm. When pressed, he confessed these beliefs to Lord Grainger and backed them up by a catalogue of half truths spun for his benefit by the Daymar household.

'Are you saying that you believe my wife is alive and well?' His Lordship asked bluntly.

'I'm afraid I am my Lord,' the Detective replied.

'And you believe Lady Daymar to be withholding the truth?'

'I do my Lord.'

Reluctantly, Lord Grainger withdrew his request for assistance from the Police but as the weeks passed, his fears turned to frustration and anger.   He took to visiting his wife's friends and relatives at unreasonable hours, badgering them remorselessly for information which, despite their protestations to the contrary, he was sure they were privy to.   His behaviour fuelled the gossips even more and eventually, he successfully alienated everyone's sympathy until even the kindest gave instructions that they were no longer 'at home' to Lord Grainger should he call.

After several weeks holed up in his study with too many bottles of brandy for company, Nanny decided to take matters in hand and bearded the lion in his den.   Several hours of straight talking from his old nurse had the desired effect. He smartened himself up and took his surprised and delighted young daughter off to play in the square.   It became a pattern for the days and weeks to come.   In fine weather, he would sit on a bench in the morning sun while Georgina played hoop and ball.   When it was cold, Georgina held his hand and side by side, they would walk silently, twice around the square before returning home.   The child was delighted to have her tall, handsome Papa spending time with her.   Even if he rarely spoke, he smiled sometimes and that was enough for her.

When Georgina was seventeen, Nanny said it was time for her charge to be presented and to have a 'coming out' debut.   Behind his closed study door, she harangued her old charge in a way that only elderly retainers are allowed.   Over the years, Lord Grainger had, at least in part, resumed his place in society but he no longer attended balls or soirées and avoided all contact with the opposite sex, unless they were relatives or servants.   He spent convivial evenings at his club with occasional forays to the gaming tables, refusing any invitation to dine unless he could be sure of an all male party; any hunting, shooting or fishing was done on his own estate.

This misogynistic state would need to end if Lord Grainger didn't want his daughter to remain a spinster for the rest of her days. Nanny, despite, or perhaps because of, her increasing frailty, wished to see her charge happily married to a suitable man and, like water on stone, dripped away at his Lordship's resolve until he capitulated.

Finally, a letter was written to his errant wife's sister, Lady Daymar, who was a socialite of the first order.   Having introduced her own daughter to the world two years earlier, she was now the contented mother-in-law to a man of wealth and position and would have leisure to arrange the same for her niece.

Lord Grainger maintained that his own sister, who also had emergent daughters, might be persuaded to include Georgina with them. But Nanny was quick to point out that Mrs. Hayford-Maine's somewhat homely faced girls would not compare favourably when placed beside Georgina's fair beauty and did not believe that any amount of sisterly love would overcome this difficulty.

'It must be Lady Daymar, my Lord. She is the obvious choice for this important task.' Nanny would brook no further opposition.

Mariella Daymar was a striking rather than a beautiful woman. She had innate style and a wealthy husband, willing to indulge her with the magnificent jewels and furs she wore with such aplomb. Few would have questioned her right to accept the sobriquet 'la belle Daymar'.

The letter from her brother-in-law, a man whom she knew detested her, was startling in its content. She paced the room, letter in hand. Finally, she took it to her husband and waited in silence as he read it. With raised eyebrows, Sir Stephen looked at his wife.

'What are you going to do?' he asked.

Mariella shrugged. 'I really don't know. It might be amusing though, don't you think?'

He was silent for a moment as he looked at her. He saw the small smile starting at the corner of her mouth. He knew that smile.

'I think,' he said, 'that by accepting this task you will take hold of a tiger by the tail. Be warned my dear, I have no intention of grabbing the other end, no matter what dire straits you find yourself in, as you will, believe me, you most assuredly will.'

The following day, Lady Daymar was ushered into the Grainger's drawing room. Father and daughter rose to greet her, one with suspicion and the other with great interest.

'My darling girl,' Mariella said. 'You are so beautiful, but what in the world are you wearing?' She looked at her brother-in-law. 'Richard, if I agree to do this, it is imperative that I have a free hand with this child's appearance. Is that understood?' She looked again at the rather dowdy gown Georgina wore and shuddered.

Lord Grainger was tight lipped. 'Do as you see fit and send me the bills,' he said, 'but heed what I say Mariella, Georgina is to be presented as the demure innocent that she is. I charge you with her good name. If it becomes tarnished in any way, I will hold you responsible and I will not suffer further hurt from your family. Do we understand each other?' His eyes were hard.

In different circumstances, Mariella would have answered with flippant sarcasm. His words were offensive and her fingers clenched into a small fist but she nodded, saying nothing as he left the room.

After so many years, Georgina found it difficult to remember exactly how Mamma had looked, but thought she could detect a slight resemblance to her mother in this stylish lady. She knew her father blamed this woman for his wife's disappearance but Nanny, even when pressed, had never agreed with him. So she smiled and trustingly placed her immediate future into her aunt's hands.

Dancing masters and music teachers were employed and were followed by dressmakers and stylists of all kinds. Georgina learned quickly and Lady Daymar was delighted with the progress of her protégée. Dressed in her new finery, Georgina was presented at court and Her Majesty not only smiled upon her but complimented her ladyship on her beautiful, well mannered charge.

A ball was planned to launch her niece into polite society and Mariella could almost taste the success. Although her own daughter was a very pretty girl she could not compare to Georgina, who was quite lovely. Also, her niece's stodgy old tutor had taught his pupil well; she was proving to be an interesting companion, with a keen intelligence and a kind, thoughtful manner, traits she had certainly not inherited through the distaff side.

Initially, Georgina returned to her home each evening and spent time in the company of her father whom she could see was very lonely. He didn't hide his dislike of Mariella but admitted that once the season was in full swing, it would be more convenient for Georgina to stay full time with her aunt until it ended. Nanny approved but made both father and daughter smile with her confusing advice as to how she should deal with over excited young beaux or rakish old roués.

On the morning of the ball, the Daymar household was in uproar, with people coming and going and the staff in a frenzy of excitement. Georgina finished her breakfast and sought refuge in her room with a good book. Her desire for peace and quiet was thwarted by the constantly raised voices, running feet and doors being banged open and shut all over the house. She decided she would leave the mayhem and go for a walk, alone.

In the hall she was greeted by the footman who suggested that as it was going to rain, he should call for the carriage and a maid to accompany her.

'Certainly not' she replied. 'I am only going to walk in the square and an umbrella will be all the protection I need.' Before he could argue, she went to the umbrella stand. The umbrellas were mostly large, black and cumbersome but in their midst and almost hidden, she saw the gleam of a slender ivory handle. She reached in and gently pulled it free. It was sadly creased but when she shook it, the fine green silk whirled and fell into soft folds.

Memories washed over her. She opened and shut it, several times, breathing in the faintest hint of perfume each time she did so. She looked at the puzzled footman. 'Whose umbrella is this?' she asked him.

'Dunno Miss, can't say as I've ever seen it before, I thought it was all gent's brollies in there.'

Georgina turned to find her Aunt watching her from the foot of the stairs. Lady Daymar was tight lipped and very still. Her face seemed drained of colour.

'Aunt, to whom does this umbrella belong?' Georgina's voice was low.

At first her aunt didn't reply but finally, in a voice higher than normal she said, 'I really have not the faintest notion, child. Do put it away there is much to be done.'

Georgina didn't move but continued to gaze steadily into her Aunt's eyes until, like a dog, Mariella was forced to look away.

'I believe it is my Mother's,' she said quietly. She looked at it again. 'In fact, I know it is my Mother's.' She moved to the door and waited for the footman to open it.

'Georgina stop! Where are you going?' Mariella was breathing fast and her eyes were wide.

'I'm going to see my father of course. Open the door please,' she said to the footman.

'Georgina, wait, please…' Mariella's voice broke.

The girl turned and looked at her Aunt. 'No,' she said at last. 'I don't believe I will.' She turned back to the door. The footman opened it and in a second she was gone, the green umbrella clutched firmly in her grasp.

Goodbye George

Ann Merrin

Well, who would have thought it? This morning started like any other: alarm; him grumping; him stomping out to the bathroom; me pretending I'm not the least bit disturbed.
Thirty years it's gone on like this. In the beginning, of course, we had a cuddle before either of us moved from our love nest and we made tea for each other. That didn't last long. It was all so gradual, this decline into miserable tolerance of each other.

I suppose the crux came when I retired. Now I don't have to move as soon as the alarm goes off. And I <u>don't</u>! That really irritated the pants off him. Ha!

'I've got another five years hard graft before I get to lie in.'
'Hard graft' my eye. He hasn't done a day's hard graft since I've known him. Office clerk for thirty-five years. No ambition, and definitely no 'hard graft'. Well, unless you count the assembly of the flat-pack bookcases. He did sweat a bit over that. It never did stand up straight.

In fact I think I can honestly say George Seaton was a totally useless individual. I wonder if anyone will notice he's gone? Well, I shall. I shall notice the distinct lack of sweaty socks in my laundry basket; the constant whining questions: where's my shirt, my socks, my shoes, my tie?… I shall miss the martyred sigh when I turn on the soaps; the inane comments when the news comes on; the ridiculous deductions being made all the way through Poirot or Morse. Oh boy, will I miss him!

I suppose I should have given the office a ring. Maybe tomorrow when I've thought about what to tell them. Maybe I should send them a letter, supposedly from him, telling Charles Henley exactly what George thinks of him and where he can stick his job. No, they may not pay his pension out. It might have been fun though.

For the moment I think I'll just have a cup of tea. And a biscuit. In fact, TWO biscuits. I don't think I've felt this good for years. I think I might go 'out' for lunch. Hear that George? Going 'out for lunch – spending money on having someone cook a meal for me AND I won't have to wash up either! Oh yes, this is going to be a good day.

I wonder if Debenhams have still got their sale on. I may get myself a new outfit after lunch. I suppose I should get something new for the funeral too. I'll make a list before I go out. Then we'll see who looks like a 'fat frump'. He really shouldn't have said that – it was just a push too far. I might get my hair done too. I'll pop into Angelo's in the High Street.

That's it, I'll have a nice day out and *then* I'll ring for the ambulance when I get back.

Favourite Chair

Patricia Welford

At the window I sit in my favourite chair
the distant hills often smudged by rain
are now heather hued ripe in the sun
uplifted I decide to make a list
of places to meet dear friends.

This task creates quite a challenge
for my stiff fingers will not write
and my mind wanders about with
memories fleeting half captured
to hover just beyond reach.

Gathering my thoughts together
I mentally place them in order
remembering highlights of my life
happy days spanning over 90 years
the birthdays weddings triumphs.

Comfy I sit musing my eyes close
I dream I've arrived in Paris
where high on the Eiffel Tower
I chat with my friends now gone
happy we admire the fabulous view.

We say good bye until tomorrow
where shall we meet next perhaps
tea in a garden somewhere hot
I smile and take their hands
let's just wait and see.

When Your Number's Up

Barbara Calvert

It had started on the day they went into town to buy Terry's new shoes: such a little thing really. The first time he keyed in the wrong pin number the assistant managed a sympathetic smile and carried on arranging the tissue paper in the shoe box.

'Oops! Have another go. Your finger probably slipped.'

Terry was pretty sure his finger hadn't slipped but he was silently grateful for her face-saving explanation. It was quite different by the time he had got it wrong for the third time. Now a queue of customers, all with lives they really wanted to get on with, was becoming noticeably restless behind him and the assistant was doing her best to maintain the company's highest standards of customer care. Terry became aware of Carol at his side, rummaging in her bag. By a stroke of luck, because she rarely carried it around with her these days, Carol had produced her cheque book with a relieved flourish and everything was smoothed over: though the smiles of relief from some of the shoppers waiting in the queue had just added to Terry's exasperation.

'Bloody pin numbers!' he'd raged as they emerged into the street. 'At least she didn't hang on to my card. I mean do I look as though I'm into some credit card scam?'

And so the following morning Terry was on the phone to his bank to set up a new pin number. Another call centre; another continent. Could they have his customer account number? No they couldn't! because he didn't know it and anyway wasn't his name, address, date of birth, even his mother's maiden name, good enough.? Apparently not. The system could only be accessed via the account number, therefore it would all have to wait until he could sort through a drawer of miscellaneous paperwork until those crucial numbers revealed themselves. Once again, that little problem was dealt with by Carol the next day, while Terry was out.

Calmness briefly returned, until the hospital appointment. Just a check-up for a procedure he'd had at least five years before. But they needed his patient number and he had no idea where that particular long-forgotten document was. He had never thought he'd need it again. Name, address, date of birth – not good enough. Nor was it good enough for the vehicle licensing authority, nor the passport office, nor the taxman. Account number, patient number, citizen number...

' I am not a number!' Carol remembered him ranting. Surely there was no other Terry Fitzgerald who was born on 25th November 1957, who lived at 73 Carnation Road and whose mother's maiden name was Stirling!

'That's who I am!' He'd yelled at the tax man, the passport office assistant and even the librarian, when she'd tried to explain the new 'computerised borrower information system'.

And so it had carried on. He'd brooded over it, he'd complained and shouted about it, he'd even started a letter to the newspaper – but Carol didn't think he'd ever posted it. And it had all come to a head the previous night. Calmly and methodically he'd gone around the house collecting up every piece of paper containing a reference number – bank statements, utility bills, National Insurance documents, even membership cards of the rugby club and the gym (long since expired). The pile grew to impressive dimensions. He'd called Carol up to his 'office'.

'That's me!' he'd announced, waving irritably at the heap of assorted bits of paper. And she had smiled. Dear old Terry!

Carol was jolted back into the present as Constable Jenny Fisher returned to the living room carrying a tray with two mugs of tea; and she'd even managed to unearth the biscuits. Was making tea after delivering bad news part of their training? Carol wondered.

'Mrs Fitzgerald, did you know there had been a little bonfire in your garden?' Constable Fisher had noticed it from the kitchen window. Carol knew nothing about it. She stood up. She needed to see this.

Constable Fisher followed her into the garden and led her to a narrow space between the shed and the garage. She pointed to a make-shift wall of bricks forming a small enclosure, inside which could still be seen a mound of grey ash and some charred remains of burnt papers. Even in this state Carol recognised it as Terry's collection of papers. He must have set the whole lot alight that morning, after she had gone to work and before he had left to go into town.

Jenny Fisher's boss, Sergeant Andy Wilson had told her, before he had left, that the driver of the van had been adamant that he'd not seen Terry walk out into the road. It hadn't taken long for a couple of Jenny's colleagues to arrive on the scene but they'd not been able to find anyone able to give a statement about what had happened. Plenty of people had been around, it was a busy street, but no-one appeared to have seen Terry before the van hit him. Strangely none of the CCTV cameras had shown any images of Terry in the area before the accident. It was as though he had never existed. As they looked down at the remains of the pathetic little bonfire Carol felt a shiver run through her body.

They went back into the house and while they drank tea Jenny dealt with the final bits of paperwork.

'Now you're sure you'll be alright?' She seemed genuinely concerned. 'I can wait a bit longer if you'd like me to.'

'I'll be fine.' Carol needed some time alone: time to try to make sense of all of this. What had really happened to Terry? Where had all this sprung from? How would she ever understand?

As they walked to the door, she assured Jenny that her son and daughter would be arriving soon.

'The folder with copies of all the information you've given me is on the table,' Jenny reminded her, 'and there's a card with all my details so that you can contact me at any time. If you can't get me just phone the station. They'll be able to help you. You'll just need to give them the incident number. It's on the front of the file.'

Lightning Source UK Ltd.
Milton Keynes UK

175077UK00001B/13/P